72 HOURS

BELLA JEWEL

St. Martin's Paperbacks

This is a work of fiction. All of the characters, organizations, and events portrayed in this novel are either products of the author's imagination or are used fictitiously.

72 HOURS

Copyright © 2017 by Bella Jewel.

All rights reserved.

For information address St. Martin's Press, 175 Fifth Avenue, New York, NY 10010.

ISBN: 978-1-250-10834-0

Our books may be purchased in bulk for promotional, educational, or business use. Please contact your local bookseller or the Macmillan Corporate and Premium Sales Department at 1-800-221-7945, ext. 5442, or by e-mail at MacmillanSpecialMarkets@macmillan.com.

Printed in the United States of America

St. Martin's Paperbacks edition / April 2017

St. Martin's Paperbacks are published by St. Martin's Press, 175 Fifth Avenue, New York, NY 10010.

10 9 8 7 6 5 4 3 2 1

PROLOGUE

Soft hazy rain falls around me, soaking my skin. My fingers glide through the damp sludge below, leaving tracks in the mud. The earth smells fresh, flowers blooming, trees relishing the shower Mother Nature has provided them for the first time in months. But for me the rain is horrible. Like a cold chill that seeps down to my very bones, soaking in and becoming a permanent fixture.

The breathing beside me is soft. It's the first time he has slept in days, I'm sure. I don't dare look, because looking means what I'm about to do will be even more cowardly. I can't bear to be a deserter, but I know that I am. I'm just not strong enough. I'm not like him. A bird chirps happily in the high trees above and I lift my head, staring through the drizzle to see it fluttering from tree to tree. If I were free, like that bird, I certainly wouldn't be flying around in *this* forest.

Death.

I can smell it, on my skin, on his, everywhere around me. It's consuming me. A shiver runs through my body as memories flood my mind. Memories I'd do best to forget; yet I know they'll *never* leave. There won't be a single second of my life when I won't see his face. When I won't hear that sound. I look back down to the earth beneath my fingers, and I curl my hand around the make-shift blade I've been holding for the last hour. It's covered in mud, but it won't matter.

It won't take long. Just a second.

A single second to escape this nightmare.

A strange sound fills my ears, and I realize it's my hysterical panting. I rub a thumb over the knife-edge, and bile rises in my throat. How did I become this? This wet, broken, cold creature on the ground, knife in hand, ready to escape the terror instead of face it? Oh, that's right. It was when my life got ripped from my hands and I was given a time frame.

Seventy-two hours to live or die.

Turns out, you can achieve a lot in seventy-two hours. Doesn't seem like much—after all, it's only three days—but when you're counting on keeping every single future beat of your heart and every breath that graces your lungs, it suddenly becomes everything you have. I wish I could say I fought for my God-given right to be on this earth, but fear has a way of making things different. Of changing who you are.

A low rumble can be heard in the distance, an alarm bell, if you will. I know what happens when it gets closer, when *he* nears. A tear trickles down my cheek as I raise the knife, glancing at a deep gash in my arm that's slowly becoming infected. It won't matter. Not now. My eyes avoid the man sleeping beside me, because, once again, I can't bear for him to see me as a coward.

The sound gets closer.

"I'm so sorry," I whisper to the sky, or maybe to myself, *probably to him*.

I don't know.

I just know I'm sorry.

So incredibly sorry for what I'm about to do.

ONE

"So, I've been dating a new guy."

I blink at my best friend, Rachel, and then shake my head. "And you didn't tell me?"

She flushes. "Well, it's only one date, but he seems really sweet. He's so cute, too."

"Details." I grin, shifting on my bar stool and sipping my drink.

"Well, he's an environmentalist."

My brows shoot up. "Like he looks after trees and stuff?"

She giggles. "I think so. Anyway, it was kind of weird because we just sort of bumped into each other and he started talking to me. He was so charming. Next thing I knew I was going out with him. He was so interested in my life, you know? Asking me about my family and friends. It was nice to be heard."

"He sounds like a keeper." I smile. "When do you see him again?"

"Soon, I hope. I didn't get his number, but he said he'd call me."

"He'll totally call you. How could he not, you're smoking!"

She laughs, but something over my shoulder catches her eye.

"Don't look now, Lara."

I glance at my best friend, who is staring over my shoulder with a tight expression on her face. I begin turning only to have her hand lash out and catch my shoulder, spinning me back around. I scowl at her, narrowing my eyes with confusion. She can be so dramatic at times.

"Seriously," she says. "Don't look. It'll only make you mad."

"What're you talking about?" I ask, pulling my shoulder free from her grip.

"Noah just walked in."

I freeze midturn, and my heart pounds so loud I can feel it in my ears. Noah. A man I haven't seen in three months, a man who has tortured my mind and owned my heart for so many years. A man who broke my heart. The very idea that I'm about to see him again sends blind terror coursing through my body. I'm not ready. Not even close.

"I didn't know he was back in town," I whisper, my voice shaky. "Where? I can't see him, Rach!"

"He is and he's not alone," Rachel says, her face sympathetic.

"What?"

It comes out as a squeak, a broken, pathetic squeak. He's not alone? He's moved on already? That hurts, more than I'm willing to admit. We didn't part on good terms, sure, but he loved me. At least, he said he did. I know I haven't been able to talk to him yet, but how could he move on so quickly? Pain explodes in my chest, and I lift my drink and take a long sip to cover it from my best friend, who is glaring in his general direction.

Deep down, I know the answer to my question. Ladies' man. That's what my friends told me when I started dating him. Not to be trusted. I should have listened.

"Do you want to go?" she asks, turning back to me. "Or do you want to talk to him?"

I glare at her.

She puts her hands up. "Sorry, I just think maybe if you two talked then things will clear up and—"

"Why should I to talk to him? How would that help?" I whisper, hurt.

Her eyes get soft. "Because I love you and you're hurting. It's been months now. I think if you talk to him, you'll be able to move on."

"He hurt me."

"I know. But you—"

"I just want to go, okay?"

She smiles sadly, accepting my decision. "Okay."

I finish my drink and start toward the back exit with Rachel by my side.

"Lara?"

I jerk at the sound of his deep, masculine voice. God, I've missed his voice, almost as much as I've missed him. I swallow the lump forming in my throat and slowly turn to see Noah standing behind me, looking down, eyes locking on mine. I shiver at the intensity in his gaze. He always had that power over me. He was the dark to my light, the hard to my soft. I might have been different when we first met, but he had this way about him that could control me like a puppet with just one look. And he's giving me that look right now.

"Noah," I say, my voice small.

His eyes flicker over my face before settling back on mine. "It's been a while."

Three months, two days, to be exact. Not like I was counting.

"Yeah."

He tilts his head to the side and studies me again. I shift uncomfortably, avoiding his eyes. He looks amazing tonight, not that I'm surprised by that. He's always towered over my tiny five-foot frame. His big body is easily six feet tall, and he's built like a statue. Muscles on every part of his perfect body. His eyes are as intense as they always were, a steel gray that pierces straight into my soul. His hair is longer than I remember, but the dark-brown locks seem even more rebellious now as they fall over his face.

"How have you been?"

I finally get the courage to look him in the eye. "Good, great."

I'm a liar.

He knows it.

"You look good, Lara."

I used to love how it sounded when he said my name, the way it rolled off his tongue. The way his husky voice coiled around it and made it his.

I hate it now.

"Thanks," I say, my voice barely above a whisper.

"I've missed you. I've been meaning to get in touch since I got back. I was hoping we could talk."

Noah told me he fell in love with me because I was sweet, sassy, and gorgeous—a rare mixture that was hard to find. He said I was the kind of woman that made a man's heart melt, that made him want to protect her and love her for as long as he possibly could, yet at the same time wasn't afraid to stand up for herself and speak her mind. At least that was how I used to be. Until I learned very quickly that doing that, being that kind of woman, would only lead to people getting hurt, or worse. There are times when I miss that version of myself. Maybe I should talk to him. Maybe I'm ready to hear him out. Maybe . . .

"Noah?"

A gorgeous blond woman sidles up beside him and I look away, unable to witness him with another girl. Even the glance I got of her has my heart ripping to shreds. The exact opposite of me.

Tall, blond, confident. Seeing her makes me realize I'm still not ready to talk to him.

"Come on," Rachel says, tugging my arm and giving Noah a look. "You don't deserve this."

Noah glares at her. "This isn't any of your business, Rachel."

"She's my friend, it's my business."

"Ah," the blonde says. "Do we know you?"

"No, you don't know me," Rachel throws in her direction. "I wouldn't bother with the likes of you. Come on, Lara. Let's go."

She takes my hand and pulls me toward the crowd that we have to make our way through to get to the door. Noah steps forward and reaches out, grabbing my arm and stopping me before we manage even five steps. Electricity runs through my body at his touch, and I want to scream, hating that it still affects me so heavily. He steps up close and I can feel him, smell him; my entire body becomes alert with his presence.

"Can't avoid me forever," he says, his voice low.

"Let me go," I plead, pulling my arm from his. "Just leave me alone, Noah."

"If you would've answered my calls and heard me out, I might've been able to leave you alone, but considering you didn't, I can't."

I spin around and finally, really, look at him. Seeing him knocks the breath from my lungs. I forgot how utterly breathtaking he is. "That's probably because I don't want to hear your excuses. I just need you to leave me alone. You're clearly busy."

"Lara . . ."

"No, Noah. Just stop."

"Lara . . ."

"Who is the woman?" I say, my voice wavering. "You want to talk to me, but it looks like you've already moved on."

"We're here meeting a friend. She's not my date," he snaps.

"You actually expect me to believe that?"

"I expect you to give me the chance to speak to you. After everything that happened with Nanna—"

His mention of Nanna reminds me of the moment I changed from being a loudmouthed, confident girl to this quiet, damaged woman I am now. Just a few years ago, I was overly confident. I was loud, boisterous, and occasionally a little too much, but I still had a good heart. Noah loved me for me, but my nanna always told me that my mouth would get me into trouble—and she was right. Except it was she who paid the price for my in-your-face attitude. After that day, I slowly lost who I was, my confidence especially. I'm no longer the woman Noah remembers.

Thinking about that night has my heart clenching.

"Maybe we should go the other way," Nanna says, *clutching my hand.*

I stare at the group of teenagers laughing and kicking over trash cans up ahead. I scoff and squeeze her hand. "No way. They're just acting like idiots. We shouldn't have to move. We'll just walk past, it'll be fine."

"Lara, I have a bad feeling about this. Let's go the other way," she pleads.

Nanna always worries. If we turn around, we're looking at adding another twenty minutes to our trip. There is no reason we shouldn't be able to walk past this group of kids without problems. I won't let anything happen to her.

"We'll be fine. They're just a bunch of kids, Nanna."

We walk toward them, paying them no attention, her hesitantly, me not so much. When they notice us, a brown-haired, scruffy teen steps forward. He looks like he's maybe seventeen, possibly a little older. His face is covered in pimples and his hair is falling over his face. He's skinny and tall, hardly threatening, but clearly cocky.

"What have we got here? Evening, ladies."

I ignore them and keep moving.

"What?" the teenager scoffs. "We're not good enough to say hello to?"

I turn and stare at him. "I wouldn't say hello to you if you were the last person on the planet and I needed to talk to you to save humanity," I say, studying him. "Now go home to bed and stop kicking trash cans around like a bunch of idiots."

"Be careful," he warns, stepping forward and in my way. "I'm not a very nice person and I don't like smart-mouthed chicks like you."

God, who does this dude think he is? I wave a hand in his face casually. "Run along and play with your toys—it's past your bedtime."

All the other boys laugh.

His face burns bright and I know I've embarrassed him. Well, that's what you get when you pick on people walking home minding their own business.

"Just stop," Nanna pleads, tugging my hand. "Just ignore them, Lara. They're not worth it. Let's go the other way."

"I don't like being spoken to like that," he says, stepping closer, puffing his chest out. No doubt for the benefit of his friends.

I let Nanna's hand go and step in front of her, crossing my arms. "Neither do I. Now, we're walking home and doing nothing, and you're causing problems where problems don't exist. Why don't you move the hell out of the way?"

"Or what?" he challenges. He's high as a kite, his eyes bloodshot. How did I not notice that before?

"Or I'll make you," I snap.

"Lara, please," Nanna begs.

"Don't upset your grannie, Lara. I can only imagine what could happen to her out here."

I bristle. "If you so much as touch a hair on her

head I'll make you wish you didn't. Now fucking move."

"I really, really don't like your mouth," he growls.

God, this guy just can't take a hint.

"And I really don't like pimply-faced, limp-dicked little teenagers who think they're cool because they can run around smoking pot and kicking trash cans over. Do you feel tough? I can almost guarantee you don't get laid and so this is the best you can do for yourself."

"Lara!" Nanna cries. "Come on."

The boy's eyes flare and he nods to his friends, who all step closer to me. Fear courses down my spine as I realize I'm surrounded. I keep my head held high and hold the boy's eyes. I won't back down for a bunch of teenagers trying to scare me.

"Please," Nanna says. "Don't hurt her. We're on our way. I have cash, if you want. Just leave us alone."

She tries to step closer but one of the boys turns and shoves her. In slow motion she falls to the ground and a loud crack radiates through the still night. Blood pours out onto the pavement around her head. "No," I scream. "Nanna!"

"Holy shit, you stupid fucker," the boy yells. "Run."

They disappear into the night and I'm already on my hands and knees, crawling toward Nanna, the skin on my knees tearing as I get closer. "Nan?" I cry, reaching her. She's covered in blood. She's *not moving. Oh God, what have I done? What the hell have I done? I take her face in my hands, shaking her gently.*

"Nanna, please wake up."

So much blood. I try to find where she hit her head, but there is so much blood I can't find anything.

A car slows and a man jumps out, I barely notice him. "I saw it all. Are you okay?"

"There were these boys," *I sob.* "One of them pushed my nanna and she's hurt. Please."

"I'm going to call nine-one-one."

"Nanna," *I sob, tears running down my cheeks.* "God, I'm so sorry."

This is all my fault. All my fault. I should have listened to her and turned around or kept walking and just been polite to them. She told me my mouth would get me into trouble one day, and she was right. What have I done? Oh God, what have I done?

"Nanna," *I sob.* "Please wake up."

Please. I'm so sorry.

I snap myself out of the memory that haunts me daily and look back to Noah, who is studying me. His eyes have softened, as though he can read my mind.

"You okay?"

"Fine," I say. "I'm going to go now."

"Were you thinking about her?"

I flinch. His eyes grow softer. He liked my nan. She was one of few people who believed he was good enough for me and wouldn't hurt me. She saw the good in Noah, and he adored her for it.

"I'm sorry, I can't do this. I have to go."

I rush out before he has the chance to say any more.

Mostly because I can't bear to hear it.

>>><<<

My eyes follow Lara as she rushes out of the
club. Her face is scrunched in pain and her tiny
form shoves through the people with a weakness
that excites me. She's timid, pathetic even. I move
my eyes to Noah, watching her go. He's a good
mix of angry and desperate. Exactly what I want.
He's looking at her like he wants to protect her
while at the same time wanting to beat her.

She frustrates him. She's fragile and weak. He's
strong and determined.

The perfect combination for my game.

The quiet little mouse and the man who will
stop at nothing to protect her.

I've been watching them long enough, setting
up my game, to know I have found the perfect
pieces. They have no idea. Not a single clue how
many times I've infiltrated their lives without their
ever knowing it. Stupid. I can't wait to see their
faces when they find out just how close I've been
all this time.

They're going to wish they never met me by the
time I'm done with them.

TWO

"Lara, can you please put my mug under the coffee machine and press START before you go for your run?" Rachel calls out.

"Already done," I call softly, leaning down to lace up my shoes.

Rachel took me in after Noah and I broke up and I moved out. I do as much as I can to help her out, including making sure she's got hot coffee every morning before I go out. She saved my ass. It's the least I can do.

"You're a gem."

So I've been told.

"I'll be back in an hour."

I grab my water bottle and move to the front door, checking that I've got my phone before heading out. The weather is warm in Orlando today, a soft breeze trickling through the trees.

After pulling my long chestnut hair into a pony-tail, I step out onto the path in front of my apartment and put my earbuds in, starting my usual morning jog. I move down two blocks and then cross a road to a local park. It has a path running beside it that goes into some thick forest before coming out close to downtown.

My one hour of peace each day.

I sing softly to the music, pounding harder and faster as my body warms up. Crossing the road, I move past the park and into the trees. The weather instantly cools without the warmth of the sun breaking through, and it dries up some of the sweat forming on my brow. I think about Noah and how much it hurt to see him at the bar last night, let alone with another woman.

Will it ever stop hurting?

A hand taps my shoulder and I scream, spinning around to see Noah standing behind me, sweat running down and soaking the front of his tank. I press a hand to my heart, studying him, then pull out my earbuds. Only he would find a way to be on his run at the same time I'm on mine. Can't this man just leave me alone? "What are you doing here, Noah?"

"I recently moved into an apartment in the area and was jogging when I saw you. I see you still enjoy running?"

"Why did you move into this area?"

He shrugs. "I liked it."

This is too much. "Why now?"

"For a while I was traveling for work. I volunteered to train some other recruits. Considering you wouldn't talk to me, I needed a distraction." He shrugs again. "Now I have a little time on my hands and it felt like time to relocate."

I take a step back, my mind reeling. "I want to finish my run," I say. "And you're going to leave me alone."

"Lara, come on," he sighs. "Let's talk about this."

I take a drink from my bottle, ignoring his pleading. My eyes focus on anything but him.

"Are you seriously still doing this?" he grunts. "I've been tryin' to call you for months with little success. You ignored me without a word and you're really not going to give me five minutes to explain?"

"Explain what?" I ask, crossing my arms. "The fact that I walked in and found you with a woman on your lap in your office?"

He jerks, and his face grows tight with frustration. "You read it wrong."

"I can't imagine how," I mumble.

He uses the back of his hand to wipe the sweat from his brow. It takes all my inner strength not to stare at his big, muscled form. Mostly to avoid remembering how good it felt to be tucked into his arms, how secure and safe he could make me feel. He just had that way. He made me feel like nothing in the world could ever touch me when I was in his arms. And then he took that all away in one moment. The only feeling of safety I had left was gone in an instant.

"Is Noah in?" I smile to the young girl sitting at the front desk of the firehouse.

"Yeah, he's in his office."

"Mind if I go through?"

"No, go for it."

I walk down the hall, heading toward Noah's office. I thought I'd bring him lunch, spend some time with him. Things have been rough in the last few months, and he's been by my side through it all. He's seen me at my worst and picked me up when I fell. After Nan died, I have felt like nothing is enough, like I'm not enough. I feel like I'm not being the girlfriend he deserves. He deserves me to try, so that's what I'm doing. I'm trying.

I open the door and step in, opening my mouth to greet him when I see her. She's on his lap, long blond hair flowing around her back, pretty as can be. The kind of woman that looks like his perfect fit. She's kissing him. Their mouths, connected, touching—it's all I see before my vision blurs, tears clouding it. I feel like I've been punched in the gut. I stumble back, gasping for air.

How could he do this to me?

I already know how. Because I'm an emotional, broken woman who got her nanna killed because she couldn't control her loud mouth. Then I became this weak, pathetic mess who spends most days crying and trying to figure out who I should be and who I am now. Of course he's with another woman. Why the hell wouldn't he be? This is exactly what I deserve.

I turn and leave, but not before I hear Noah call out my name.

I run, tears flowing down my cheeks.

"Lara!" he calls. "Lara, wait!"

He catches me at the door, hand curling around my upper arm. He spins me around but I shove at his chest, causing him to stumble backward.

"Don't touch me!" I scream. "Don't touch me."

"Lara, it isn't—"

"Get away from me."

I turn and keep going, darting straight across the road. I reach the park and drop to my knees, sobbing with agony, and pain, and regret. Maybe this is my karma. Maybe this is the universe's way of punishing me for what happened with my nanna. Or maybe, just maybe, Noah is better off without me.

Of course he is.

I'm worth nothing.

"Lara, fuck, how could you throw it all away? We were together over two years."

His question brings me back to the present. "Seriously?" I ask, eyes wide with shock. "You think *I'm* the one who threw it away?"

God, if only he knew how much it meant to me. I wanted to marry this man, to have kids with him, to be with him for the rest of my life. Walking in and seeing him with another woman ripped my heart out. It sent my whole world crashing down. Leaving him was the hardest thing I've ever had to endure in my life. How he could think it meant nothing is beyond me. He was the one who hurt me.

He grunts. "Yet you won't talk to me, you just broke it off and ran."

I flinch. "It was what I had to do."

He shakes his head, jaw tight. "God, you're a pain in the ass."

That hurts. He's acting as if all this is my fault, when it was he who cheated on me.

"I don't need to listen to this, Noah. I don't deserve it."

"That's just the thing," he yells. "You're not listening. You're refusing to listen."

The familiar sting of anger bubbles in my chest, but I push it down. *Be calm. Don't react. It isn't worth getting upset over.* "I don't want to hear your excuses."

He makes a frustrated noise in his throat.

I shake my head. I can't listen to any more of this. I can't take any more of this. "I have to go." I turn my back to him and start walking away.

"Fuck, Lara," he barks. "Let me talk to you."

I pick up into a jog and disappear out the other side of the trees, but not before I hear his angry curse. I run until I'm out of breath, but I could swear he's still behind me. I stop and turn every now and then, glancing into the trees, but nobody is there. Yet it feels as though someone is. He's probably following me—he's protective like that, always wanting to know I'm safe. He doesn't need to worry anymore—I'm no longer his burden.

THREE

I avoid jogging down my usual path for the next week, hoping to avoid running into Noah again at all costs. He's tried to call a few times, but I figure he's learned by now it doesn't matter how much he calls because I won't answer. I have nothing to say. I'm trying to move on with my life.

"Ma'am, the line has moved forward."

I jerk out of my thoughts and shuffle ahead in the Starbucks line I've been waiting in for the last ten minutes. It's my job to get coffee for my work colleagues every day. So I spend close to half an hour in here every day because I am forced to come at peak time. I don't mind, though; it lets me drift off into my own little world where no one bothers me.

"Sorry," I mumble to the man behind me.

I reach the front of the line after another five minutes.

"What can I get for you?" the sour young man says, clearly bored with his day already. Is it so much to ask for good customer service these days?

"Two grande cappuccinos, two grande lattes, one venti iced coffee."

He nods and scribbles it onto the cups with my name and I move to the group waiting for the drinks to be made. The girls behind the counter are in no hurry either, chatting happily about their weekends and the men they're dating, taking their sweet time to make the drinks that everyone is waiting for.

"Morning."

The voice comes from behind me, and I turn and see a middle-aged man sitting at a table just to my left. I glance around, not sure if he's talking to me, but realize that he's looking directly at me. Maybe he's confused, or maybe he's just friendly. That would be a nice change. "Ah, morning." I smile shyly.

"Long wait, isn't it?"

I nod. "It is."

"You doing the morning run for your workplace?"

I laugh softly. "Is it that obvious?"

He smiles. He's good looking. Blond hair, blue eyes, all-American-boy smile. He seems like the type of man Rachel would swoon over.

"It's always the quiet ones," he says, almost to himself.

I give him another smile and turn back to the line.

"Do you work around here?"

Why is he talking to me? People don't usually make the effort to talk to me, because I tend to keep my head down. "Just up the road at the Morgan and Francis law firm," I mumble.

He nods. "I've heard good things about them."

I shrug. "I'm just a receptionist."

He smiles. "You don't seem like the type to be just a receptionist."

"I guess you read me wrong."

His smile widens. "I never read people wrong."

Okay.

"Lara."

The sound of Noah's voice to my left has me spinning around. He stands in the line, studying me. God, it's as if I can't escape him. This is borderline stalking now. He's probably following me. He's a take-action kind of man and if he wants something, he gets it. Still, if he thinks I'm going to give him the satisfaction of talking to him, he can look elsewhere. I'm not going to listen to what he has to say.

"Did you follow me here, too?" I ask.

He narrows his eyes. "I like coffee, and it's close to my new job. I don't think that's considered following you."

I clench my teeth but say nothing.

He looks good today. He's been a firefighter for six years. He started as a volunteer years ago but quickly became chief. His job is his life. It works for him. It suits him. A good portion of the women in Starbucks are staring at him, and I can't blame them. He's wearing a tight black tee but it's the yellow pants slung low around his hips, dirty from wear, that make him irresistible. They're probably seriously considering lighting their houses on fire just to get him to save them.

I can't say I blame them.

"We can do this every day or you can just talk to me and then I'll leave you alone if you want," he says, moving closer and leaning down so his voice is close to my ear. I shiver at the hot breath that tickles my neck.

He's leaning down close, way too close.

I take a step to the side. "I've told you there's nothing to say."

He growls, low in his chest. "God, you fucking drive me crazy. Why can't you just hear me out?"

I swallow but say nothing. I collect my coffee and leave.

I need a damned vacation.

I walk out of work later that night, tired from a long day. It's dark out and the streetlight shines down just over my car, which is comfortably parked a little too close to the curb. I'm looking forward to going home and getting some sleep.

My mind is a complete mess at the moment and frankly, I'm ready to get away from it all.

From him.

"Lara."

I exhale loudly. For the past three months, I thought I'd never see him again, and now I see him every single time I think about him. I turn slowly and see Noah leaning against a lamppost, arms crossed, studying me.

"There's a law against stalking, Noah," I say, pulling my keys from my purse.

He pushes off the post and walks toward me. "I'm not stalking you, I was just waiting for you to finish work so we could talk."

"What part of *I don't want to* are you not grasping?" I mumble, unlocking my car.

He steps forward as I go to pull my door open and presses his body against mine, putting his hand on the roof of my car and effectively trapping me.

"Noah," I breathe, going weak at the very feeling of him pressing against me.

"We're going to talk."

I hate that he thinks he can dictate what we will and will not do. I used to love that about him. Now I hate it.

"No," I say, trying to shove him away so I can open my door and leave.

"Lara," he sighs. "You left me, moved out without a word, shut down for months, and didn't give me one second of your time. I left for training,

I called but didn't push. I wanted to give you time, because I respected that you needed it. Now I'm done waiting. We're talking."

"No, we're not."

"Jesus, when did you get so damned stubborn and unreasonable?"

That just makes me angrier, but I squash it down and take a deep, shaky breath. "I'm not ready for this and I don't think I'll ever be. Now get off me, Noah, or I'll scream."

"Seriously?" he says, exasperated. "Why the hell would you do that?"

I twist so I'm facing him, then tilt my head back and look up. "Because you hurt me and I've asked you to leave me alone. You're choosing not to respect that and I'm tired of it."

His eyes hold me. "When did you start to hate me so much? God, we went through so much together with your nan and you just leave me without an explanation?"

"Without an explanation?" I cry, my emotions taking over. "You were kissing another woman!"

"It wasn't what you think, you should have known me better. I'd never do anything to hurt you. If you had let me explain, you'd know that. Stop using your insecurities as a barrier, Lara. You know me."

I flinch.

My insecurities. Another consequence of losing Nan. When I first met Noah, I never thought twice about being good enough. The day I lost Nan was the day the confidence floated away, as if she took it with her when she died. I became a shell of a person. I stopped loving who I was, yet Noah stood beside me. He held my hand through it all, through the ups and downs, through the pain and heartache. Through the change in who I was. Yet it only confirmed my feelings that I wasn't good enough for him. He loved me, I knew that, but I knew it was a matter of time before he'd go looking for more.

"Get off me Noah," I say, my voice weak, tired.

"Come on, Lara," he rasps. "It's me. Stop the act, you know I'd never hurt you."

"I don't know a damned thing," I snap. "All I know is what I saw. I saw you with a woman on your lap, and she was kissing you. And the sad part is, I know what I became—why you would have wanted her—so you don't need to explain anything."

"My God," he growls, seeming to finally crack and let a little of his anger show. "You have no fucking idea, do you?"

"Just leave me alone, *please*."

"Lara, fuck . . ."

"I don't want to talk to you, Noah, now leave me alone."

"No," he growls. "For once in your life you're going to stop with the fucking games."

Games?

Is he serious?

That both stings and makes me angry.

"Get off me, now!" I yell, which is pathetic even to my ears.

"Ma'am, is everything okay here?"

I look past Noah to see a police officer standing, glaring at Noah. I shouldn't do it, I shouldn't, but I just want to be left the hell alone. I'm trying to move on and he's making it impossible for me. Memories of that woman in his arms flitter through my mind and push me to open my mouth and say, "No, it's not okay. He won't get off me."

The pain and anger in Noah's eyes as he looks at me with utter horror and shock break my heart.

I turn my head to the side and look away.

"You know what," he says, pushing off me. "You're not worth it."

Those words wound me more than I could have ever imagined.

* * * * *

The tension is there, ready and waiting.

*The more she rejects him, the angrier he gets.
That's exactly how I want him: irritated and
exasperated.*

*He needs to have resentment. It's vital to my
plan.*

*I'm going to encourage that along, and I know
just how to do it.*

*My game won't be nearly as satisfying if they
work together. He needs to be livid.*

She needs to be weak and broken, fragile even.

Then my game will be ready to be played.

FOUR

"Let me buy you a drink, beautiful girl."

I stare at the attractive man standing beside me at the bar, eyes on mine, smile planted on his perfect face. I'm in here sulking. It's been a week since I saw Noah last and I feel worse with every passing second. I don't want to admit that a small part of me liked seeing him so much after three months of not seeing him at all. So I'm in here, trying to drink my sorrows away. So far, it's not working.

"Me?" I ask, sure he must be talking to someone else.

I look like a wreck. Hair in a messy bun. No makeup. Faded halter top and jeans. "Yes, you. You're alone, it looks like you could use some company."

"Oh," I laugh softly. "I'm waiting for a friend."

That's not a lie. Rachel promised she'd meet me after she finished work.

"Then you have time to let me buy you a drink. I promise I don't bite."

He smiles, a genuine, warm smile, and it feels nice to have someone looking at me like that again. Someone who doesn't know me. So I do what I wouldn't usually do.

"Okay," I say softly. "Vodka and soda, please."

"As you wish."

He orders the drinks and turns to me while they're being made. "What's your name, beautiful girl?"

I touch my hair self-consciously. "Lara."

"I love a woman who's naturally gorgeous." His eyes twinkle. "I'm Marco, but you can call me Marc."

"It's nice to meet you, Marc."

The bartender slides us our drinks, and Marco hands mine to me. "What are you doing alone here on a Friday night?"

I shrug, nervously sipping my drink. It's been a while since I've been chatted up by a stranger, and I feel incredibly awkward.

"My friend and I meet here every Friday night," I tell him, taking another sip.

"Why here?"

I shrug again. "We met here."

"Ah, I see. What do you do for a living?"

I stare at him. He's so open, so comfortable in his own skin. He should be, too. He looks like a

Greek god. He's got dark hair, dark-brown eyes, and olive skin. His body is muscled but lean. He holds himself well; he oozes confidence.

"I'm a receptionist," I say. "Nothing too fancy."

"I hear they have the hardest job?"

I laugh softly. "Yeah, I would say I do sometimes. What about you, what do you do?"

"I work for a shipping company. Nothing spectacular."

"Have you lived here long?"

"All my life."

We ease into an easy conversation about his personal history, his family, and his work. He asks me questions and the more drinks I have, the more at ease I feel talking to him. When I realize Rachel hasn't arrived, I pull out my cell and excuse myself, dialing her number. She doesn't answer. That's odd. She would let me know if she couldn't make it, and so far she's well over an hour late.

I go back to Marco after shooting her a quick text, and he's gotten me a fresh drink. "Would it be too forward if I asked you to join me for something to eat?"

I study him.

He wants to take me out?

I haven't been out with anyone since Noah. I haven't wanted to. Going out with someone else might be nice, possibly even good for me. I've held on to a love that I can't trust for the last few months. Maybe it's time to let that go. To let him go. The thought of really releasing Noah from my life hurts more than I'm willing to admit, especially considering I hurt him last time we were together. Maybe we are both better off without each other. Why does that thought kill me inside? I push down the pain and smile. "Sure, I'd like that."

"Well, finish up the drink and we'll go for a walk. There are some great places around here."

I do as he requests, finishing my drink. Then I grab my coat off the chair and check my phone as we exit the bar. Still nothing from Rachel. Odd. Maybe she got held up at work, or stuck in a meeting where she can't answer the phone. I fall into step beside Marco and we walk across the road toward the park I usually go jogging past.

"Do you live around here?" Marco asks as we near the trees.

"Yes, just a few blocks up."

"Any suggestions for a good eating spot?"

My head feels a little light. Surely the alcohol isn't affecting me this heavily so soon?

"There's a great little café through these trees and out the other side, closer to the city."

"Sounds good to me."

We move into the trees, small lamps lighting the path we walk down. I stumble a little, which is odd. I really didn't think I had that much to drink. Still, I laugh at Marco's jokes and talk freely with him, all my inhibitions seeming to have flown out the door. We're near the middle of the thick trees when Marco stops and turns to me.

"It's nice in here, isn't it?"

I turn, stumbling a little and facing him. My head feels so light I actually lift my hand and make sure it's still there, then laugh hysterically because of course it's still there. I try to focus on Marco, but he's blurring in and out. Have I been drugged? Is that what's happening? God, did Marco drug me?

"I know it sounds forward, but I'd really love to kiss you," Marco murmurs, cupping my face and moving toward me.

His lips touch mine and I don't even try to pull back, not because I don't want to, but because my body just doesn't seem to want to play the game. I reach up, curling my fingers around his biceps, to push him away, but I seem weaker than usual. His kiss gets more intense, and I can't seem to find the strength to argue.

I hate it. After kissing Noah, no man could ever compare.

The lightness in my head has moved over my whole body and I feel like I'm flying. My knees wobble, but Marco holds me up with an arm around my waist, kissing me deeper. He's getting a little too intense now.

"Seriously?"

The voice seems almost distant, but I recognize it instantly. Noah.

"Let her go or I'll make you," Noah warns.

"Hey, man," Marco says, pulling back from me but keeping his arm around me. "Don't know who you are, but this is my girl."

His girl? Wait, what?

"Are you fuckin' serious?" Noah barks, looking to me. "Lara, what the fuck?"

This whole scene feels incredibly confusing. Why is Noah here? Am I dreaming this whole thing?

As I try to make sense of it all, I curl an arm around Marco's middle to try to hold myself up.

"So that's how it is, huh, Lara?" he spits out. I open my mouth to reply but can't seem to form any words.

What the hell is wrong with me?

Noah shakes his head. "I thought we had a chance, but now I see how stupid I've been. It's really over."

He sounds broken.

My heart twists. I don't want him to give up. I've been pushing him away but deep down, inside the parts I won't let out, the idea of him leaving rips me to shreds. I wish I could tell him, but no sound will come out of my mouth.

"You should leave now," Marco says, and my head starts spinning.

He holds me tighter.

"No. Don't leave yet. The fun has only just begun."

A voice. I can hear it; I can't see the person who owns it. I blink and try to focus past my blurred vision, but it's too difficult. A dark shadow comes up behind Noah; I can't make out his features. Is it even a person? Maybe it's a tree. My head spins again. I think I'm going to be sick.

"Who the fuck are—"

Noah's words are cut off and the sounds of grunting fill the silent night. Then his body hits the ground—his big, beautiful body just falls. I start struggling against Marco, confused and disoriented. My struggles are futile; I barely manage to get my body to move. The shadowy figure comes closer. I can't make out his face, only his white, straight teeth.

"Ready to play, Lara?"

Something sharp stings in my neck.

Then my world goes black.

FIVE

FIVE

Damp earth is pressed against my back.

That's the first thing that alerts me to the fact that something is not right.

The second is the soft rain falling on my skin, drops gathering and then rolling off my cheeks. I try to open my eyes, but my eyelids are heavy, weighing me down and refusing to allow me movement. When I wiggle my fingers, soft mud squelches through them and panic seizes my chest. What the hell?

I struggle to remember what went on the night before. In fact, I have no memory of it at all. I struggle to think back to my last clear recollection—it was me texting Rachel earlier in the day to organize our usual Friday drinks. Everything after that is a blur. I focus on my eyes again, taking a deep breath and opening them. Cloudy sky greets my hazy vision, and I raise a hand to rub until that vision clears.

I'm in some sort of forest.

Did I go for a run and pass out?

I move my hands down to my clothes: jeans and a halter top, heels on my feet. No. Not a run. I focus back on the thick trees covering most of the sky, allowing only patches to peek through. They're no match for the incessant drizzle, though. It manages to make its way through and hits my skin like a soft mist. I look to my left—nothing but trees for miles.

I look to my right, and freeze.

Noah is sitting against a tree, eyes closed, one eyelid swollen and red. His head is slightly drooped and he's soaked. I take another steadying breath and push up to a sitting position. I'm covered in mud, and my head is pounding.

Where the hell are we? Why is Noah here? Worse, why is he hurt? I check myself over but find no wounds.

"Noah?" I croak, my voice dry and thick.

He doesn't move.

Is he dead?

Fear crushes my chest, and I force my tired body to move closer to his until I can reach out for his face. My fingers gaze over the stubble on his cheeks, then move to his puffy, swollen eye. It's grazed by light scratches. Did he fall over? My hand moves down to his shoulder and I shake him gently. "Noah."

His hand lashes out so quickly I don't have time to pull back. He gasps and his eyes fly open. He twists my arm and I scream, tumbling forward. A painful crunch in my shoulder alerts me to the fact that my arm didn't move with me. Noah, as if realizing what he's doing, suddenly lets me go. His chest rises and falls with heavy pants as he looks around.

"No," he rasps. "Fucking *no*."

"Noah," I whimper, rubbing my shoulder. "What's going on?"

His eyes dart backward and forward and then land on me rubbing my shoulder. "I hurt you."

It's not a question.

I shrug anyway.

"I didn't realize it was you . . ."

I'm confused. "Who did you think it was?"

His jaw tenses. "How long have you been awake?"

"A few minutes. What's going on?"

He starts fumbling with his clothes, arching his hips up and shoving his hands into his pockets.

"Noah?"

He ignores me, coming up with a folded piece of paper. He clenches his eyes closed and mutters a curse before unfolding it.

"What's going on?" I prompt again.

"I'm prayin' it isn't what I think, what I remember . . ."

He stares down at the letter, and his entire body goes solid. Something fills the air, and if I didn't know better, I would say it's fear. What could Noah be afraid of? He's scared of nothing.

Something is very wrong.

"Please explain to me what the hell is going on," I beg.

He looks up at me. "You don't remember anything?"

I shake my head.

"Not a thing?"

"No, Noah," I cry, frustrated. "No. Is this some sort of game to get me here so we can talk, because if it is, it isn't funny."

He glares at me. "You're kidding?"

"Well, nothing else seems to make any sense. You've been hassling me to talk to you—"

He makes a growling sound in his chest. "Don't insult me. This has nothing to do with us. Do you honestly not remember seeing me last night with your little fucking boyfriend?"

I flinch. "Pardon?"

He shakes his head, bitter smile on his face. "Drugs removed that, did they?"

What the hell is he talking about? "What drugs? What boyfriend? What are you talking about?"

"Playing coy used to be cute, Lara," he snarls. "It isn't anymore."

"Will you just tell me what's going on?"

His eyes meet and hold mine, and the look in them is scaring me. "We've been captured."

I'm sorry. Did he just say *captured*?

I study him, eyes wide. "What?"

"I didn't stutter," he replies, thrusting the letter at me. "I remember bits and pieces. There was a note on my windshield this morning from you saying to meet you in that park. After what you did last time I saw you, I thought it was over. But then I got the note and thought you were finally ready to talk to me. I went in and you were there with another guy. Someone else came in and I think drugged us. Whatever drug he gave me wasn't strong enough and I woke up a few times. Heard him mumbling about his game, and how close it was. He sounded like he was going to fuck himself with excitement before I passed out again. Then I woke up and we were out here. I freaked out, you were passed out . . . couldn't wake you."

"A note?" I say, confused.

"You didn't put it there, did you?" he says, his voice tight.

"No," I whisper. At least, I don't remember putting a note on his windshield.

"So somebody wanted us to be in the same place at the same time," he mumbles.

"What's going on?" I whisper.

He reaches into his pocket and pulls out a note. "This is what I found in my pocket just now."

With trembling hands, I take the note and unfold it, reading words that send a chill up my spine.

Welcome Lara and Noah,

How wonderful to have you here. You're probably wondering why you're so special. Why are you good enough to play? Why did I pick you?

Well, if I revealed everything at once, it wouldn't be a game, now, would it?

Let me get to it. I tend to ramble when I'm excited.

And I am excited, you see.

I've been planning for this moment my entire life, down to every fine detail. I even studied personality traits. How clever of me, don't you think? It seems like a miracle, really, that you two were thrust into my hands. All this time and you never even knew I was there. But I was there. Always watching. Waiting.

My players.

My game is quite simple. You won't forget the rules, because there are none. But, like all good and fair games, I need to give you a head start. It wouldn't be right if I won without even a little fun, would it? No. Of course not.

Seventy-two hours.

Such a special number to me. It took seventy-two hours for my mother to bleed out when I sliced her entire body, the cuts just big enough for a gentle trickle of blood to escape from each wound, for her to writhe in agony as she prayed for death to take her. The human body can be quite a miraculous thing: It constantly tries to save us, even when there is no hope.

But that's a story for another day.

You get seventy-two hours to prepare yourselves for my game. You can do whatever you want; there are no boundaries. Once your seventy-two

*hours are up, I'll come for you, and, like the good
little players you are, you'll make it fun for me.
You'll run. You'll hide. You'll fight. You'll try to
escape.*

But you can't.

You won't.

I've made sure of it.

*I'll hunt you until I finally decide to kill you
both. I have great plans for how I'll do that, but it
won't be a surprise if I tell you now. Just know—I
like to play with my prey.*

I wonder how you'll make use of your time?

Tick tock.

I thrust the note onto the ground and push to
my feet. "Is this some sort of joke?"

Noah stares at me, then pushes to his feet as
well. "I don't know. I'm not entirely sure I'm willing to risk it not being a joke. If seventy-two hours
is all we have, I'm not wasting it playing guessing
games."

"This is a joke," I laugh hysterically. "It's someone trying to prank us. You can come out now,
you got us!"

Not a single thing moves.

"Seriously, there has to be a way out."

Noah scowls at me. "I walked a few miles in
each direction when you were sleeping. Wherever
he dumped us, it just keeps going."

I spin around to face him. "That doesn't mean
it's not a joke. I mean, this can't be real. It's too
insane."

He laughs bitterly. "Tell me, Lara. Which of your friends would think it's funny to drug us, throw us in a dense forest, and leave us in the cold rain?"

Goddammit.

No.

I try to think of another explanation for how we got here and who might have written the note, but nothing adds up. God. What the hell is happening?

"Noah, there has to be another explanation."

Noah steps forward, running a hand through his hair. "When you come up with one, I'd love to hear it. Until then, I'm taking it very fucking seriously because I heard the man driving when we were out of it and I can tell you, he wasn't right in the fucking head."

My voice shakes when I speak next so that my words come out scared and frantic. "Maybe it's some sort of reality TV show or—"

Noah gives me a scornful expression. "Don't be stupid, Lara. There is no fucking way it's a reality show. They can't do a single thing without a million forms being signed."

"These things don't happen in real life!" I cry, panic rising in my chest, heart pounding so hard I can barely think past it.

"Clearly you don't watch the news."

I clutch my hair. Vomit rises in my throat, and I drop to my knees and throw up. There is barely anything in my stomach, but whatever is there comes rushing back out. I feel like a tight fist is clutching my heart, and I can hardly breathe.

"This can't be happening."

"I wish for the same, but it is, and as far as I know, this freak is very serious."

I look up at him, tears running down my face. "We're in the hands of a serial killer?"

"Wouldn't call him that, though I can't be sure he's never done this before. Still, from the sounds of it, he's been planning this awhile and he's been watching us. This man isn't a serial killer, he's a fucking psycho."

I gag.

"All we have is seventy-two hours before this psycho fuck comes after us, so we need to move. If it's a joke, we still need to move. Either way, in a few days it'll be all over or our nightmare will have just begun."

I shake my head so fast my teeth chatter together. "No, I'm not moving. I'm not."

If we move, we could end up anywhere. We should be staying where we are—we're more likely to be found. Isn't that how this works?

"We should stay here," I continue. "Where we can be found."

Noah growls low in his chest and takes a step toward me. "Trust me, we're not getting found. I'm not waiting around to die and I'm not going to leave you. Either you move or I'll make you."

"Why us?" I scream.

"This is exactly why." He waves a hand around

angrily. "Look at us. We are a broken mess. Now stand."

I shake my head.

"Fuckin' stand!" he barks.

I flinch and tears roll down my cheeks. I don't want to stand. I want it all to go away. I want to close my eyes and just make it go away.

"Goddammit, Lara. That sick fuck will be sitting there enjoying every second of this."

"He can see us?" I cry, eyes frantically darting around the forest.

God, is he really watching us? How? I don't understand? My heart pounds as I study the trees, the sky, hell, even the birds. My heart feels like it's going to leap from my throat as my eyes take in our surroundings. How would anyone set something like this up? Why would they even want to? How long would it have taken him to create such horror? No. No.

"If he's been planning this for as long as he says he has, and is so sure we can't escape, then you're damned right he can see us."

"How?"

Noah studies the trees. "Haven't figured that out, but I'm going to because I don't feel like dying. Now get up."

I nod and push to my feet, tossing my heels, because he's right, I can't sit in the same spot and risk doing nothing. What help I'll be to him in the state I'm in, I don't know, but if there is a chance we can get out, I'm taking it.

Noah takes my arm roughly and pulls me through the trees. He's angry at me. That's not going to help anything, but arguing with him right now is only going to make things worse and at the moment, I need him here with me.

So long as he's with me it'll all be okay.

Please don't leave me.

>>>|<<<

It's working exactly how I wanted it to.

He's so angry at her. She's showing the fragile, broken side I've been counting on her showing.

But he'll protect her. It's in his nature to at least try. And that's how I'll break him down.

It's how I'll make my game satisfying.

I laugh hysterically. My game. Finally coming to life.

I never thought I'd see the day. I've worked so long and so hard. And these two are the perfect couple, like they were thrust into my hands, like the earth planted them in the right place at the right time just for me.

They say everything happens for a reason, right? Too bad reason is a person, just like me. Imagine that—the world isn't as pretty as people think!

Otherwise these two wouldn't be here, looking like scared, lost little puppies.

Oh yes, my game is going to be incredible.

And the best part is, I can change the rules whenever I want.

Oh, they're in for a treat.

SIX

We walk for what seems like miles and miles, yet we don't seem to be going anywhere. I swear I keep seeing the same trees over and over. I've sobbed myself dry. Fear is now sitting in my chest, refusing to leave, crossing its happy little legs and singing an annoying song that'll taunt me for every single second we're here.

It still doesn't feel real.

They say when something so absurd, so unrealistic happens, it's human nature to wonder if it's real. It's in our nature to question it, to come up with a thousand different scenarios as to why it happens, because the cold hard reality just can't be real. I feel like that right now. Even as the hours pass and nobody comes out and tells us it's just a joke, even as we walk and walk, tired and sore, even as the day rolls on and night prepares to fall. It just doesn't seem real.

Like there must be some other logical explanation.

I read, a lot. I've read about serial killers, I've read good thrillers and romantic suspense, but that's all it is . . . *fiction*. It's created to entertain an active mind. It's no more than a creative author putting words onto paper. Those things don't actually happen. I know the world is a vile and hideous place at times, but this . . . *no*.

"You need to keep up, Lara," Noah barks, jerking me from my thoughts.

"I'm doing the best I can," I say, my voice tired. "We've been walking most of the day."

He spins around to face me, arms crossing over his big chest. "Would you rather we sit and wait to be killed?"

My bottom lip trembles. "Don't, Noah. I'm scared, too."

"There is only one way out of this mess, and it's to find a way ourselves. This man is clever, but no plan is without flaws."

"Well, wherever we are, we can safely say no one is around."

"Wrong," Noah says, shoving a thick branch out of the way and letting me past. "This man has to be close enough to be able to hunt, to carry out whatever sick game he's come up with, which means there has to be a way in and out."

I scoff. "Isn't that what we've been looking for this whole time? A way out?"

He glares at me.

I look down at my feet, now void of shoes because nobody can walk through a forest in heels.

He leans in close. "Listen, Lara, I might not read a thousand fucking books but I'm not stupid, either."

"I never said you were," I say softly.

He steps back, spinning around and stalking forward again. "I'm going to figure this out, but considering we've already wasted a day, time is of the essence."

"If we walk until we're exhausted, we'll never be able to come up against whatever plans this man has for us," I offer carefully.

He stops, rubbing the sweat off his brow with the back of his hand. "I know that, but he isn't stupid. I've seen a few coconut trees around, and a stream, which means he's made sure we can find food and water. He doesn't want us weak—that wouldn't be any good for his game. The man is smart, he knows eventually we'll stop and eat, rest and heal ourselves, because we're not stupid. He's counting on that."

That makes sense, total sense, even if I don't want to admit it. He wants us strong; he wants us to be a good challenge. That's why he picked us. He thinks he's got us pegged, he thinks he knows our ins and outs. Maybe he does. I don't know. I don't know anything anymore.

Bile rises in my stomach and I stop, pressing a hand against the bark of a thick, rough tree.

Breathe. In and out.

"He's made it easy," Noah goes on, ignoring me. "But he hasn't made it entirely untroubled. He's provided us with water, but we are walking most of the day so we have to figure out how to take it with us, considering we've only passed one small stream. He's provided us with coconut palms, but they're high and difficult. Nothing is without strain."

I nod, wrapping an arm around my middle, trying to stay calm as bitter reality sets in.

"I know this isn't easy, Lara, but you need to get yourself together."

Fury takes over and I jerk my head up. "Get myself together?" I scream, shocking even myself. "We're in a forest with a psycho watching us, waiting to come in and kill us, and you're telling me to get myself together?"

"Yeah," he says, his voice cool and calm. "That's exactly what I'm telling you."

"I don't want to die like this, Noah!"

He flinches, then storms over, grabbing my shoulders and jerking me up close. "We're not going to die. Do you hear me?"

"You think he hasn't thought of every escape route? Or every possible scenario? Do you think he would have put us in here if he wasn't a hundred percent sure that we couldn't get out? That

he could find us and hunt us? Jesus, Noah. Whoever he is, he hasn't just done this on a whim."

"Hey," Noah growls, shaking me a little. "You
might be right, but are you going to sit here and
give up or are you going to fight? There might be
no chance, but I'm still certain that whoever he is,
I can find a way to beat him."

"He's probably got weapons not even you can
come up against."

"Again," Noah snaps, "stop with the negativity.
If we're going to die, we're going to do it fighting
to live. Do you understand me?"

I nod, but I can't stop the tears from leaking out
of my eyes.

"Lara, you're upset and scared, which is making
you doubt everything. He's counting on that. I don't
know how you're going to do it, or where you're
going to find it, but you need to find the strength
that I know you have buried deep inside you to
stand up and fight with me. If you don't, we're
doomed before we even begin."

"Strength?" I whisper. "I don't know how."

He steps back and waves a hand. "You have to
find it, or you'll die. What's it going to be? I know
you've got it in you, we *both* know that. You need
to dig down and find it again, or we won't walk
out of here alive."

He's hit me right where it hurts. He's talking
about the girl I was before Nan. I don't have it in
me to tell him that she's already dead.

Night falls and with it comes eerie silence and complete darkness that terrify me. Noah finds a small overhanging tree that we sit under. We stopped at a stream and had some water, but neither of us felt energetic enough to climb a tree or figure out how to get the coconuts down. We decided we'd do that in the morning; for now, we're here and we're together. Not that we're talking, but we're together and that has to count for something . . . right?

It's May in Florida, so the nights are still a bit cool. Not cold enough that we'll freeze, but on a good, clear day it can get chilly enough at night to need a light coat. Tonight is still partially overcast, so the weather is cool but not cold. I press my back against a tree and rub my hands over my bare arms, wishing I'd worn a sweater out the evening before.

Noah hasn't said a word to me in hours and it's killing me. He told me to be tough, to find my strength, yet he's refusing to make conversation with me—and when he does speak, it's only to spit acid at me. How we're supposed to work together to get ourselves out of this horror is beyond me. I rub the back of my neck where a dull ache has started to form, wondering if it's from whatever drug we were given.

I can't see Noah in the dark, but I know his face must be sore; he hasn't complained, though, so I've chosen not to bring it up. I can feel him next to me, his big, warm body close enough that the heat gently caresses my skin, but not close enough that we're making any kind of contact. I exhale and run through a million scenarios in my head, like I've been doing all day. I try to put myself in the mind of this man, try to figure out what I can about what he's got planned, but I just can't seem to piece anything together.

I can't remember a damned thing from the night before, and it's frustrating as hell. Maybe if I could, I'd be able to figure out who put us here.

"You cold?" Noah asks, finally speaking. His voice is gruff, tired, maybe a little scared.

He'll never show it. It's not in his nature. Noah will fight until his last breath, because that's the kind of man he is.

"Not really," I say, even though my arms are a little chilly.

"Take my shirt, it'll keep you warm."

"No, you keep it on. It's not that cold."

"Then at least move closer so you can get some of my body heat. We might not be getting along, but the point of the matter is we need to get out of here alive."

I don't argue. I move closer until our shoulders touch. It is a lot warmer.

"Why do you think he picked us?" I ask softly, tucking my knees up to my chest.

"Best I can figure is it's because we don't get along," he mutters. "If we already drive each other to the brink of madness, we're doing exactly what he wants. Playing right into his game."

"But why us? Why not another dysfunctional couple?"

"Wrong place at the wrong time."

It can't be that simple, surely. No, someone who planned something this detailed wouldn't just pick two randoms. The thought that he's been watching us, for God knows how long, makes my skin crawl.

I chew on my lower lip. "I'm sorry, Noah."

"For what?"

"That I've handled this so badly, acted so weak and pathetic."

Noah doesn't answer.

That feels like a punch to the stomach.

"You're not pathetic or weak," he finally says, his voice low and thick. "You're lost and confused, you don't know who you are anymore. There's a difference."

I'm not sure it's a good one. And his words still sting a little, despite his reassurance, because I don't think he is right. He saw what I went through with Nan. He saw how that affected me. I had to change who I was, because being who I was got people hurt. I'm not lost and confused, I'm just a different person.

"I'm scared I can't survive out here," I say softly.

It's not a question, but a statement of fact.

"So am I," Noah says, his voice quiet.

That's not what I expected him to say. He must be getting tired, I realize. He's not only contending with an unthinkable situation, but dealing with me, too. Am I going to be the reason we don't make it out of here alive? Am I going to let Noah down? Myself? What if Noah gets hurt because I'm not able to handle whatever is coming? Maybe they're all wrong. Maybe I can handle it. Maybe I'll have no choice.

"I'm not going to stop fighting," I say softly. "I know my emotions have been scattered today, but I'm not going to stop fighting."

"It isn't about the fight, Lara. It's about so much more than that.

"He's going to target the weaknesses that are obvious in you. You can fight, that's a given, but you can't handle violence anymore, you scare easily, and he's counting on that. If I'm right, he's going to target me to weaken and torture you."

"I won't let him," I say defiantly. "I'll figure it out, but I won't let him, Noah."

He huffs into the dark. "You can't change who you are, Lara."

I fall silent.

"You and I both know I can."

He has no answer to that.

"Do you have any idea what we're going to do?" I ask, changing the subject after a few minutes of silence.

"I'm still trying to figure it out. I don't know how it is he's watching us, but I can guarantee he is."

"Do you think he can hear us, too?"

"Oh, the fucker can hear us. Probably sitting

there wanking his dick right now with joy. Stupid fuck."

I swallow. How can someone hear us, see us, and yet we don't know about it? Every plan we make, everything we talk about, he's always going to be one step ahead of us.

"So how do we outsmart someone we can't get out of our heads?" I question.

Noah leans in close, so close I shiver. He moves the hair off my neck and whispers so softly I can barely hear it, "Not even the best technology can hear this."

I tremble, because his breath on my neck has sparks running down my spine and settling into my core. I close my eyes and swallow, then nod and pull away.

Neither of us says anything after that.

Because what is there to say?

I bring the coffee to my lips, my hands trembling with utter joy as I watch them fall asleep next to each other.

His body is tense. He knows I can see him and hear him. He just doesn't know how and it's killing him.

He's that kind of man. He likes control. He likes to know he's got everything covered, and he can't figure me out.

More than that, he's angry. At me. At himself, but mostly at her. He's trying not to be, but he is. He's like a simmering pot, slowly bubbling away until eventually he is going to explode.

And when they fight, they do exactly what I want.

He makes her doubt. Makes her feel bad. Makes her self-esteem dip even lower. I don't need to break her down; he'll be doing it for me.

And he'll know I'm doing it, but he won't be able to help himself.

A chuckle escapes my lips. Two more days, my players, and we'll begin.

Just two more days.

SEVEN

I fall asleep against Noah, head on his shoulder, body semi-warm from his skin. I must be exhausted, or maybe I'm still coming down from the drugs still in my system, but I don't move all night long.

I'm woken in the morning by Noah shifting and the sounds of birds chirping high above me. I blink a few times, rubbing my eyes and focusing. We're still against the tree, but Noah's arm is around me now, holding me close. We're still here. This isn't a dream. A horrible lump forms in my throat and my heart sinks. I try to fight back my tears as realization slams into my body. I don't know what I thought, but a part of me hoped I'd wake up today and it'd all be over.

I squirm out of Noah's grip, and he does nothing to stop me.

I push to my feet, needing to use the bathroom.

I move past Noah without a word and find a tree to settle behind. A flittering thought comes into my mind: Is he watching even this? I choose to pretend he isn't. The sun is out today, the rain clouds having disappeared. I'm not sure if that's a good or a bad thing.

I don't know what Noah's plans are, but the clock is ticking. We only have today and tomorrow left before our world turns into a nightmare. We need to figure something out before then—or better yet find a way out of this hellhole. I finish up going to the bathroom and make my way back to Noah. He's studying the trees, the ground, anything that moves. He's like a hawk, eyes zooming in on anything out of the ordinary.

"What exactly are we looking for today?" I ask.

My stomach makes a loud rumbling sound and I realize, despite it all, I'm hungry.

"First, food," he mutters, not looking at me. "Then we're going to see if we can find a boundary, maybe get an idea of where we are. We need weapons; I'll have to make them but it's better than having nothing."

"Weapons? How are we going to get those?"

"It's not hard to make a knife from a piece of solid wood, a few sharp rocks, and a steady hand. It will do the job."

God.

I'm not hungry anymore. The sickness is back.

"Let's find the stream. There were some coconut palms close by. Come on."

We walk in silence through the forest for about an hour until we come to a small stream with clear water trickling through it. It isn't deep, probably not even deep enough to bathe in, but it seems to go on for miles. I wonder if it leads to something bigger, deeper maybe? We use it to wash our faces and our bodies; then we cup our hands and drink as much as we can. Noah studies the trees, squinting to see what we've got to work with.

"Sick fuck," he mutters.

I look up. "What?"

"I'm just pissed that he gave us the one food source that is hardest to get. Coconut palms."

"Are coconuts all we've got?"

"Yeah," he grunts.

He walks over to the palm tree and starts shaking it, his big body pulling the thin base back and forth. The coconuts don't budge. Growling with frustration, he finds a big stick and starts hitting it, over and over until his muscles are bunching and his face is an angry red. He looks beautiful like that, so masculine and strong. I hate myself for that thought. It should be the last thing I think about.

"Do you want me to climb another tree and see if I can reach over and shake it, or get a coconut?"

He stops shaking the tree and looks at me. "If I don't have to risk you getting hurt right now, I won't. I'll get one."

"But—"

He ignores me and keeps shaking the tree.

Giving up on that, he finds a big rock and throws it. I expect him to miss, but he hits one of the coconuts square-on and it drops from the tree. He lets it fall before going over and picking it up. He shakes it, nods, and then walks over to a log lying across the ground, an old tree that's snapped. He puts the coconut on the log, then starts hunting around for a sharp rock.

I feel helpless.

While he uses a rock to peel the first layer of the coconut, I wander around, trying to find something to carry water. There is very little. Nothing that is deep enough, strong enough, or durable enough to hold water for any amount of time. Frustrated, I kick some old shriveled green coconuts around. Then it hits me. We might not be able to carry large amounts of water, but we can carry enough to get us by until we come across another stream by simply using an empty coconut. I lift four and bundle them into my arms, walking back to Noah.

"Can we put a hole in the tops of these?"

He lifts his head from the coconut he's peeling and studies me. "They're probably old. We can't eat them, Lara. I would have picked them up already if we could."

"I know that," I say, my voice peevish. "I was thinking of emptying the contents by making a hole and filling them with water to carry."

His brows go up.

"So do you have the strength or the right equipment to make a hole in the tops of these?"

"It'll take a while, but yeah. Put them down next to me and come over here. You can crack this while I put a hole in them."

I walk over, dropping the coconuts, and extend my hand for the one he's already peeled right down to the little brown ball in the middle.

"Find a sharp rock, a stick, whatever you need to use and hit it until it cracks open."

I nod, taking it from his hand and walking around until I find a sharp, jagged rock poking out of the ground. I lift the coconut and bring it down over the rock. Not a single thing happens. Frustrated, I do it again, and again, and before I know it I'm slamming the coconut on the rock, anger bubbling in my chest, rage coursing through my veins.

What the hell is happening to me?

With a pained cry, I hit it harder and harder, crying out when it won't break. I slam it down again and again until my shoulders ache with strain.

"Hey," Noah says, stopping me with a hand to my shoulder. He pulls me back. "Slow down, Lara. Fuck."

He takes the coconut from me and effortlessly brings it down over the rock. It splits first. That makes me angrier. I turn and scream into the forest. "This is complete and utter bullshit! We're being hunted by a psycho killer," I scream, "and I can't even crack a fucking coconut!"

Noah doesn't say a word, and when I turn around, he's studying me. Our eyes meet and my breath catches in my lungs. He's looking at me like it's the first time he's seen me in a long time. Or maybe it's the first time he's really truly seen me. His face is soft, his eyes are intense, and he hands the coconut back to me.

Just before he turns his back to me, he says in a soft voice, "I was wondering when the Lara I knew would show herself. Keep it there, Lara. On the surface. We might just have a chance of escaping if you do."

My heart twists and I swallow the lump in my throat.

He turns and goes back to doing what he was doing, but I'm standing there, my body numb.

We fill the coconuts with water after a solid two hours of stabbing sharp items like rocks and sticks into them to make a hole big enough. It works in the end, and we fill our bellies with water before refilling and carrying them with us. We eat one coconut and take another with us. Noah tells me to drink the water from the middle of one; apparently it's hydrating.

You learn something new every day when you're being stalked by a psycho.

We walk for hours on end and my feet have gone from sore to numb. I no longer feel the sharp rocks and jagged edges of the sticks stabbing into my skin as we venture deeper and deeper into the thick shrubbery surrounding us. The trees that were once mostly spread out are now squashed together and surrounded by tiny bushes. There is a small poorly formed track worn through and I have no doubt who created that.

Noah and I argue about it, because I say the smart thing would to be to go off the man-made track and into the forest, but Noah tells me that we'll barely get a mile through those thick trees before we're exhausted from shoving and cutting branches. He claims that Psycho—as we've dubbed him—made it so we're almost forced to stick with his created track.

Whatever.

At least it takes our minds off the looming reality that we only have one more day after this. And so far we've found nothing. No way out. No sign of life. Zero. Nothing. Noah is frustrated, and he's letting it show. He swears at every second tree and spends a majority of his time in brooding silence. I can't really blame him; I know he's suffering. We both are. If we don't find some way out soon, we'll die.

It's that simple.

Afternoon hits like a painful reminder, but we keep walking, keeping our eyes peeled, looking for some sort of end to this wilderness, maybe a sign of life. Anything to give us hope. When the sun starts to lower on the horizon, we face our worst fears. We're pushing through the forest, not speaking, both of us exhausted, when we come into a small clearing; ahead is a fence. It's not any old fence. It's big, super high, and topped with barbed wire. But it's a fence.

"It's a fence!" I scream, running toward it. "Look, Noah, a fence!"

Freedom. Escape. We just have to get over it. I'll cut my own leg off if it means I get out of here. I'll do anything. Relief floods my heart and tears run down my cheeks as I charge toward it.

"No," Noah roars. "Lara, stop!"

Stop? Why the hell would I stop? There is a fence. He must have lost his mind. My heart pounds and I pump my feet harder, shoving trees out of the way, leaping over logs, and running like I'm being chased. I'm about three feet away when a hard arm wraps around my waist and hauls me backward. Before I know what's happening I land on my back on top of Noah's chest, his arm still around me. He makes a loud *oomph* and rolls us to the side.

"What the hell are you doing?" I screech. "Jesus, Noah."

"Do you want to fucking die?" he bellows, flipping me over so I'm on my back and his big body is looming over me.

"What are you talking about? Let me go," I cry, squirming. "It's freedom. It's a way out."

"It's pumped with electricity, Lara. Jesus Christ, you just about fried yourself."

I blink. "What?"

"It's electrified in a big way. Fuck, can't you hear it?"

I go silent. Beyond my breathing and pounding heart, I can hear the *tick tick* of the fence. Everything comes crashing back down, all my hopes, all the freedom I felt, the relief—it slams back into my body and all I feel is the piercing sting of disappointment. God, we're never getting out of here. With every step we take, it feels like there isn't a single thing we can do about escaping.

Keep fighting. At least try.

I close my eyes and lift my face up to press into his hard chest.

"We're going to be okay," he says, cupping the back of my head and holding me against him. "We're going to find a way out, Lara."

"There doesn't seem to be a way out, Noah."

"Then we'll kill the fucker."

I flinch. "Noah . . ."

"If fighting is all we have left, then that's what we'll do. I haven't seen a single fucking way out of this place, so the only option is to fight. There are plenty of logs and rocks we can use to carve weapons. It's not over, Lara."

Fear courses down my spine. "Yes, you're right—but what if that's not enough?"

"Look at me," he demands.

I drop my head from his chest, meeting his eyes. "I won't let anything happen to you, do you understand?"

I nod, taking a shaky breath.

"I won't leave you alone out here."

I know I should believe him, but I don't know what the hell I believe anymore.

I just hold his eyes, and something inside me

sparks to life. This man, whoever he is, put Noah
and me out here thinking we'd make things harder
on each other, but he was wrong. Noah and I,
we're not going to let this beat us. I lick my bottom lip and move my eyes away from his, because
if I stare into them a second longer I'm going to
do something I shouldn't. Seeing this side of Noah
takes me back to the way he was with me when
we first met. God, he protected me so fiercely.

"I'm going to get another drink." I smile, lean-
ing up and kissing Noah's lips.

*"Okay, baby, don't be long. That dress, those
shoes, you'll have the entire bar looking as soon as
you step out of my arms,"* he growls into my ear.

*I shiver and smile up at him. He's so beautiful.
Perfect in every way. I love him so fiercely.*

"I won't be long."

*I turn and saunter through the crowd, stopping
at the bar. To my left are two men, who stop talking
the second I lean over the solid wooden counter
and order my drink. I glance at them and they're
both looking at me, leering. Ugh. When did men
become so blatant? Whatever happened to actually talking to a girl before checking her out?*

"I won't be long," the bartender tells me.

I nod and smile.

"Hi there."

*I smother an eye roll and turn to see the man
closer to me, smiling. He's not handsome, but he's
not terrible, either. Just your average Joe. It's always the average Joes that are the biggest creeps.*

I'm not entirely sure why, but they seem to think they're God's gift to women.

"I'm taken," I say, turning back to the counter.

"Whoa, I was just saying hello."

"We both know you weren't," I mutter.

"I like a challenge."

I turn and glare at him. "I don't. Now go bother someone else. I'm taken."

He reaches over, taking a strand of my free-flowing hair into his hands and tugging it enough to make it sting. "Sassy little thing, aren't you."

Another hand comes into the picture, curling around his wrist and twisting. A harsh cry leaves his mouth and he looks up at the same time I do. Noah is standing there, angry expression on his face, hand wrapped so tightly around the other guy's wrist that his face is going quickly red with pain.

"Why the fuck do you have your hand on my woman?"

"I was just, ah, she had something in her hair, man," the other man squeaks.

"Funny, I'm certain I heard her tell you to go away. So why"—Noah leans in close, twisting his hand even more—"the fuck didn't you go away?"

"Sorry, man. No harm meant."

Noah twists harder and the man cries out, bottom lip shaking with pain.

"I suggest you leave. Right fuckin' now."

Noah lets him go and he stumbles off the bar stool with his friend. When they're gone, he turns to me. I reach up, grabbing his face and crushing

*his lips against mine. I kiss him deep and I kiss
him hard.*

*"I love it when you get all caveman," I murmur
against his mouth.*

Noah pushes off me and stands, snapping me
from my memory. He runs his hands through his
hair, and I glance away awkwardly. He leaves his
back to me for a few minutes before turning
around and reaching out for my hand. I hesitantly
take it, and he pulls me to my feet. "We've got tonight and one more day before this fucking crazy
lunatic comes after us. We need a plan, Lara. Let's
find somewhere to stay for the night and work out
what we're going to do next."

I nod. I have no other words. My memory has
stirred up hidden emotions inside me, emotions I
thought I was doing a good job of keeping con-
cealed.

I guess not.

He keeps hold of my hand and pulls me back
into the thick forest.

I turn and watch the fence disappear from my
view, my heart sinking a little more with every step.

I just don't know if we're going to get out of
here alive.

I laugh hysterically as he tackles her to the ground.

Granted, I don't want her to die that quickly, but the very idea that she might have leapt onto that fence and cooked herself is such a good thought, I can't help but wish it had happened.

Imagine the look on his face if she had the life ripped out of her by a fence. I mean, how hilarious would that have been?

He's all macho, trying to protect her, and she goes and runs into an electric fence.

I laugh again.

God, she's so fucking stupid. She just doesn't think. It'll get her killed, that I'm certain of.

Oh wait, I'm certain because I'm going to be the one to kill her.

I think I might just kill her first. I'm starting to think Noah will make for a very interesting game when she's gone.

The decisions. Oh the decisions.

EIGHT

We find a small overhanging rock and decide it'll be the best we can find before sundown. We fill our coconuts at a passing stream and then find ourselves a comfortable spot on the ground, close to each other for warmth. Noah's big thigh is pressed against mine, and it's so warm I want to shuffle closer. My heart pounds being this close to him, and my pathetic, weak side is begging me to climb onto his lap and find the comfort I so desperately need. My stubborn side is refusing to give in that easily.

I feel guilty for having that thought. I shouldn't be so stubborn. Maybe, just maybe, it's what got me into this mess in the first place.

I'm beginning to see that I've been going about this all wrong. I've been shutting Noah out because I couldn't bear to hear that he didn't want me anymore, that I wasn't good enough for him. It was my punishment for getting Nan killed. But now, being around him, seeing him these past few weeks, I've realized how much I've missed him and am ready to hear his story.

But people aren't mind readers. They don't know when you're wishing with everything in your body that they'd touch you, or pull you into their arms, or kiss you. Noah has always been an open man, always affectionate with that edge of broody.

And tomorrow could likely be my last day on this earth. What have I achieved?

My heart breaks.

"Noah?" I croak, voice small and weak.

"Yeah?"

"That day I walked in, and that woman was on your lap. What happened?"

He goes silent for so long, I wonder if he's fallen asleep or hasn't heard me.

"You choose now to ask?" he mutters.

I exhale a shaky breath. "We might die, that's the cold hard truth of this situation. I never gave you a chance to explain and that wasn't fair, I know that now. I think I need to hear it."

He makes a sound in the back of his throat, but starts speaking. "Her name was Amy and she used to come in and help out with paperwork at the fire station, as you know. She had a crush on me, I knew that but I didn't think she'd do anything. That day she came in and was delivering her usual weekly report and she just walked over and threw herself onto my lap. She kissed me and to be honest, I was in fucking shock. I had no idea what to do."

"And I walked in," I whisper.

"You walked in. It was one of those moments you see in a movie, or read about. You picked that exact moment to walk in and see her on my lap kissing me. I wasn't kissing her back, Lara. I might be a lot of things, but I'd never, not fucking ever, cheat on you."

A tear rolls down my cheek.

I screwed up.

I lost the love of my life, because of my own insecurity.

"I'm sorry, Noah," I manage. "That'll never be enough, I know that. I was so fucked up. So sure I didn't deserve you after what happened with Nan. I was in such a bad place. You saw me at my worst. You saw me being ripped open and stuffed back together all wrong. When I saw that woman on your lap, I felt like that was my punishment, like I deserved that, like you deserved that. I just didn't think I was enough for you. That's the damned truth. So I ran, without thought, without waiting. I just ran. It was easier."

"Fuck," he mutters. "Fuck, Lara. Do you think I would have gone through all that with you after your nan if I didn't think you were everything I needed? I fucking loved you. I deserved a chance to explain."

He was so incredible after Nan died. How

could I forget how wonderful he was? If it weren't for him, I don't think I would have gotten through those months.

I'm sitting by the window, staring out, tears running down my face. I cry more than anything these days, but every single time I think of Nan, I can't stop the flow of emotion that runs down my face. A strong hand curls around my shoulder and I turn, looking up to see Noah staring down at me, his expression soft.

"I hate seeing you cry, baby."

He sits down, pulling me onto his lap. I tuck myself into him, the only comfort I have left. I don't deserve someone as good as him. I don't deserve anyone.

"It hurts so much," I sob. "I can't make it go away."

"You have to let it go, Lara. You didn't do anything wrong."

"I killed her!"

"No, a bunch of teenagers high on drugs did."

"If it weren't for my smart mouth, we would have never even gotten into that mess. You know that. Nothing you can say will change that."

"Right now, I know that's what you believe so I'm not going to give you words to try to change it. Instead I'm going to tell you I love you, I believe in you, and I think you're a good person. One mistake does not define you, beautiful girl."

"I'm not beautiful, Noah. I'm a monster."

He holds me close. "You'll never be anything

*but beautiful to me. I won't give up on you, Lara.
I'm going to get you through this. I swear it."*

"I know," I whisper, fighting back the emotion
from the memory. "I know you did."

It's not enough, it'll never be enough, but it's the
only thing I can think to say.

"That man you were with," he says, changing
the subject. "The night we got taken . . . it fuckin'
killed me."

"What man?" I ask, shuffling through my memories to try to figure out what he's talking about.
It's all a blur. I recall meeting a man at the bar, but
it's all hazy and I don't recall what we even spoke
about.

"The one you were kissing."

I blink. "Pardon me?"

"You don't remember?"

I shake my head. "I remember meeting a man
while I was waiting for Rachel and having a drink
with him, but I still can't remember anything from
after that point. I honestly don't."

He curses under his breath. "I thought something was off with you. Fuck, you must've been
drugged even before the psycho came along."

"What?" I squeak, voice rising.

"The night we got taken, you were with a guy
claiming to be your man. You were playing along,
and fuck, I believed it and it hurt."

I can't remember anything about that, and frustration bubbles in my chest.

"I don't . . . remember."

"It doesn't matter."

I go quiet, still digging through my memories to try to figure out what the hell happened. It's blank.

"That's why you're so angry at me."

It's not a question, but a statement.

"It wasn't just that. You disappeared on me. It took me months to find you. When I finally did, you nearly got me arrested. You hurt me, Lara."

I close my eyes, even though he can't see it. "You hurt me, too."

He grunts.

"If we'd had this conversation earlier, we might not be here," I say, with full understanding that my stubbornness and insecurity quite possibly put us in this situation.

"Don't," he warns. "Like I said earlier, if it wasn't us, it would be someone else. We were in the wrong place at the wrong time, and that isn't going to change. No point dwelling on the past."

"I really am sorry I didn't give you the chance to explain."

"You broke me. You moved out of our home and just walked away, shut down and refused to talk to me. It wasn't even a real breakup. It messed with my head. I needed to talk to you, and I couldn't. So I went to training and when I came back and had to get a new place, I told myself I had to accept that we were over. But I just couldn't move on. I needed to try at least one more time."

My heart twists.

"I screwed up. Seems I'm good at that."

He reaches over and surprises me by taking my hand. "Wouldn't be human if you didn't screw up. Maybe this is your chance to stop blaming yourself for fucked-up shit other people do, and for not being able to change the past. Because guess what, Lara? No one can. Everyone has regrets but you can't let them destroy you. You just have to learn from them and do better next time."

Did it really take us being kidnapped to finally sort through our problems?

I tremble.

"You cold?" he asks.

"No," I say, my voice low. "I'm terrified."

He reaches over and effortlessly lifts me onto his lap, nestling me in, putting me against him where I fit so perfectly. His big arms go around me and I press my cheek to his chest. I love this man. I've loved him since the first moment I met him. Charming, gorgeous, a little scary. He was my complete opposite, yet we worked in a way that didn't make sense to anyone but us.

"Do you remember when we first met?" I whisper against his shirt.

His heart beats against my cheek. I love how that feels.

"Yeah," he chuckles, low. "Fuck, that was the best night of my life."

I close my eyes on a smile, and remember the moment I laid eyes on him.

"Don't look now," Rachel cries. *"But there is a super-hot man staring at your booty."*

I flush. "What?"

"Yep, he's giving you a look like he wants to fuck you right here, right now."

My cheeks grow pink and I turn, glancing at the man sitting at the bar, eyes on me. I've had men look at me in my time, but never like this. His gaze is smoldering and he's looking at me like he's about to come over and throw me over his shoulder. He doesn't hesitate as he drags his gaze down my body. Openly. Without shame.

I turn back to Rachel. "Why is he looking at me like I'm a piece of meat? How rude!"

She giggles. "It's not rude, he thinks you're hot."

"He doesn't even know me," I huff. "I'm going to ask him to stop."

"Oh, you do that, just let me get a drink and watch this one play out."

I take a deep breath and approach the man still staring at me. His mouth twitches when I near and it only makes me angrier. How dare he sit there and openly ogle me. Seriously. I'm not a piece of ass. I could be married, for Christ's sake. As I get closer, I realize that he is, in fact, extremely good looking. He's also big, like really big. Muscled and ripped. My throat gets tight as I stop in front of him.

"Excuse me, I'd appreciate if you'd stop staring at me. It's making my friend and me uncomfortable."

His lip quirk turns into a grin. "That so?"

"Yes that's so. It's rude to stare at women like you want to take them away and eat them alive."

A full-blown smile now. "Eat them alive? Is that what you want me to do with you?"

I bristle. "It is not. No. I don't . . . I don't . . ."

A flash of white teeth. "Do I make you nervous, little one?"

"No you do n-n-n-not," I stammer. God, no one ever makes me nervous and this man is making me stammer? What has gotten into me?

He chuckles. "Cute, aren't you, honey?"

I flush. "Just stop . . . stop staring at me."

"I'm enjoying the view. It's a free country."

"It's rude," I say, my voice trembling.

He leans in close. "Admit it," he says, his breath tickling my ear. "You're thoroughly enjoying it."

"As much as I'd enjoy being poked in the eye with a fork."

He laughs, deep and sexy. Damn. Damn him.

"We're done here," I say, stepping back. "Knock it off and learn some manners."

"Or what?"

"Or, I'll . . . be unhappy."

There's that grin again.

"Whatever," I mutter, turning and attempting to rush off, but I trip and stumble into the bar, catching it to steady myself.

The man stands and walks over, leaning down and helping me up, a grin on his smug face. "I'm taking you on a date," he says, slipping his number into my palm. "Call me, or I'll find you."

I open my mouth to argue, but his big hand is so warm against my arm that I can't concentrate.

When I'm safely back on my feet, he leans in and brushes his lips against my cheek before whispering, "Make sure you call me. I'm very good at tracking down what I want."

Oh boy.

"You were so fucking flustered, it was adorable," he says, snapping me out of my memory. "When you told me to stop because you'd be unhappy, I knew I had to have you. I could tell that you normally had all the confidence. I knew I'd gotten to you when you stammered."

My cheeks heat.

"God, I embarrassed myself so hard that night."

"Cutest thing I ever saw. This little gorgeous woman trying to tell a big guy like me to stop looking at her. You were trying so hard to sound serious."

"I was serious," I protest.

"You loved every second of it."

I huff. "I did not like being ogled like that. Women don't like that."

He puts a hand on my knee and squeezes gently. "No, you loved it but didn't want to admit it, and that's exactly why I knew I was going to chase you. You were so different from all the other women I'd met, who all threw themselves at me. You had confidence and an independent spirit. You just came over there and gave me a piece of your mind in the fuckin' cutest way. I was hooked."

"I'm not cute."

He squeezes me. "Try as you might, you'll always be cute, baby."

Baby.

I shiver.

"Imagine what he's thinking right now," I whisper into Noah's ear. "Seeing us like this?"

Noah turns and presses his mouth to my ear. "I think he's crapping himself, because he's betting on us working against each other."

"We'll show him."

"Yeah, Lara, we'll show him."

I hope he's right.

No.

What's happening? What the hell is happening? They're not meant to make up.

They're not meant to work with each other. He's supposed to hate her. She's supposed to cower.

Frustration and desperation battle in my chest. This is my game, goddammit. My fucking game. They don't choose how this goes.

She leans in and says something to him. Why can't I hear her? What's she saying? Why is he smiling?

I launch out of my chair and take my keys. I'm going to find out. I know they have a few more hours to go, but nobody is going to ruin this plan.

I've worked my entire life for this. If those fuckers think they can get away with turning it around on me, they're wrong.

So very wrong.

NINE

I wish I could say it's the cold that wakes me, or even the sun shining through the trees, but it isn't either of those. It's dark, so dark I can't see much, but I can hear just fine. It's the rustling that rouses me. I quickly realize that it isn't Noah, because I'm still tucked into his side and I can hear his soft breathing beside me.

Someone else is here.

My body is frozen. I can't move. I don't even want to. Footsteps come close, close enough to make my breath seize in my lungs, refusing to escape. I have to act like I'm asleep. I have to pretend. Noah starts snoring softly. He has no idea that someone is standing right next to us. Is this it? Is he going to kill us? No, it hasn't been seventy-two hours yet. No. He wants the game, he does.

So why is he here?

I keep my eyes closed and try to appear asleep

even though my entire body is screaming in fear. *Don't tremble. Stay still. Try to breathe.* A few seconds pass. It feels like minutes, but eventually the footsteps move away. I open my eyes just enough to see a soft light near the tree to my left. I can see it without moving from Noah's chest.

I can make out the outline of a man. He's tall, not overly bulky. I can't see his hair color, or even his features, but he doesn't look threatening from here. I suppose anyone can be a threat with a weapon, but alone not many people are actually that terrifying. A scary thought. I blink a few times, keeping my breathing even, and watch as the man reaches into a tree.

What the hell is he doing?

He fiddles around for a few minutes and then comes out with something in his hand. Goddammit, I can't see what he's got. I squint. Nothing. He does something else then returns the item to the tree, high enough that whatever it is can't be seen at normal eye level. What the hell would someone put on a tree? What could he be checking?

Then it clicks.

A camera.

My body stiffens and I'm forced to take a few stuttering breaths to relax myself again. It makes perfect sense: He's got cameras in the trees. He needs to be able to see us wherever we are and so he's created a situation where we've been forced to stay on his path, because going into the dense underbrush would simply be too hard. It would take hours to move even half a mile, plus it would be impossible to see snakes and other venomous creatures. So we've been following his predetermined route this whole time. Playing right into his hands. God, how long would it have taken him to wire up cameras in the trees?

I watch for a few more seconds as he looks back at us. I shut my eyes, praying he didn't see me with them open. The flashlight moves past our heads. I don't move. I don't even breathe. A second later it's gone, and I can hear retreating footsteps.

I lie like that for well over an hour, needing to be sure he's gone before gently turning my body as if I'm just moving in my sleep. I move my mouth to Noah's ear and whisper, "Noah, wake up."

He doesn't move.

"Noah," I whisper again.

He shifts and groans, then his voice comes out husky. "Lara?"

"Don't speak out loud," I whisper frantically. "Pretend I'm asleep."

"Lara, are you awake?" he says.

I don't move.

He shifts into position so we're face-to-face. Neither of us moves.

"What's going on?" he whispers.

"He was here."

His entire body stiffens. "What?"

"I woke up, and he was here. I didn't move. He didn't know I was awake, but I saw him doing something to a tree. Noah, I think he has cameras in them."

Noah curses under his breath. "Fuck, of course he does. I've been trying to figure out how he'd find us after the seventy-two hours are up. I thought he must be watching from a distance. Setting up a massive network of cameras seemed too involved."

"It took him a while to get the camera out. He fiddled with it then put it back."

"If he's watching us from those cameras, then we need to be out of range," Noah whispers, squeezing me closer.

"So we go off his path?"

Noah shakes his head. "No. We'll never get far in there; it's so overgrown, we'll barely be able to move, let alone run. He's not stupid. He's cleared only the areas he wants us to use because he knows we're not going to get far in the interior."

"So what now?"

"I don't know yet," he whispers, frustrated.

"We've walked for miles. How many cameras could he have put in?"

"We've also re-trekked a lot of the same ground because of those fences. He must have us blocked in a certain area. He's been planning this for so long, he's probably got cameras everywhere."

"That's a lot of cameras."

"Don't underestimate the mind of a killer, Lara."

"So what do we do?"

"We can't go into the forest, so that leaves only one choice," he whispers, pressing his mouth to my ear. "We go higher than them."

Higher than them.

We climb the trees.

Could it truly be that simple?

TEN

Morning comes like a nightmare.

Our last day before he comes after us. We both know it.

Even after the events of last night, we're both very aware that by this time tomorrow we're going to be running like hunted animals. I can't eat. I can't even drink. Fear has lodged itself into my body and I can't shake it. Gone is the nausea, the crying, the terrified chatter. I'm just silent, legs tucked to my chest, back to the tree, unable to make my body function.

I don't want to die.

I don't want to be hunted.

My chest clenches and my skin prickles at the very thought.

"Hey," Noah says, squatting down in front of me, studying my face.

He looks scared, too, but he's holding it to-gether. He's stronger than me.

"Lara, look at me."

I meet his eyes.

"We're going to get out of this."

"Are we?" I whisper, and even that's shaky.

"Yeah, we are, but you need to stay with me. You can't shut down now, you can't close in on yourself. I need you, and you have to be strong. Can you do that for me?"

I nod.

He glances at something over my head, then leans in and whispers, "You were right, he's got one hell of a setup going on in these trees. We're going to climb them, and he's going to see us doing that, but at least we might have a chance of throw-ing him off our scent."

"When are we going to do that?" I whisper back.

"This afternoon. But first, we're going to make weapons. I need your help with that, so you have to get up and get yourself in the right frame of mind for me, okay?"

"I don't think I can," I whimper.

"Lara," he growls, his voice firm. "I will be hard if I have to, if it makes you move your ass. You need to get the fuck up, do you hear me?"

I start to cry. He's right. I know he is, but it's hard to find the strength he needs from me. I haven't been that girl in a while. And this situation is beyond every horror I've ever imagined. I feel myself crumbling.

"Up," he orders, standing. "Get up."

Is doing any of this worth it? "Noah," I sob.

"Get up," he bellows.

I get up.

Somehow I push to my feet and walk toward him. He takes my shoulders, shaking me softly. "You gotta find your strength. I know it's in there. Find it. You have to find it or you're going to die before tomorrow is over."

I make a terrified sound in my throat.

"Find it, Lara."

Find it.

Find it.

I have to find it.

"I'll find it," I say, meeting his eyes. "For you, for me. I'll find it, Noah."

He cups my jaw and then, without warning, he brings his lips down over mine. It takes me by surprise and for a few seconds I just stand there, legs trembling, body unable to move. Then I kiss him back. I give it all I've got. His strength pours into me, lifting me high, taking me to the level I need to get through this. Our tongues clash, our bodies press together, and our lips move like we never spent a single day apart.

With a groan, he pulls me closer, hand on my lower back. Our bodies fit together, big and small, strong and fragile. He lifts me up enough that my feet dangle just off the ground. I wrap my arms around his neck and give him everything I've got to give, because the reality is I might never know what it's like to kiss Noah again.

He pulls back after a few seconds and stares down at me, running his thumb over my swollen bottom lip. "We've got this."

"We've got this," I repeat.

Then he turns his head to the cameras in the trees. "You'll crash and burn, fucker. You can be sure of that."

I hope whoever is behind those cameras is squirming right now knowing that Noah and I are in this together.

Noah lets me go and when my feet touch the ground, I feel stronger, like maybe with this man beside me I can get through this.

"What do I need to do?" I ask.

"Go and find the thickest branches you can, the sharpest rocks, anything you think can be used as a weapon. We'll carry it on us so it can't be too big."

I nod and turn, disappearing down the rugged path. I venture off for a moment or two and realize very quickly that Noah is right. The path is rough, but off to the sides is a mess. There's no getting through the thick stands of trees covered in dense layers of vines. The trees do space out in some places, and we might be able to use those places to hide, but we wouldn't be a safe distance from the path.

I push branches out of the way, looking for sharp objects. I manage to come up with a few thick branches that have snapped off and a few lethal-looking rocks. I carry as much as I can back to the little camp we set up. Noah is sitting on a fallen log, using a rock to carve a stick. He's made a sharp end that looks like it would easily glide through someone. I take another piece of wood and a rock, then I sit beside him and start doing the same.

By the afternoon we have three spears, two knives, and five sharp rocks that not even I would want to mess with. My fingers are raw from carving and I have splinters, but I feel a little safer now. These weapons might not do much against a killer, but they leave us with a whole lot more than nothing.

"We're going to wash our clothes today, fill more coconuts and put them in the trees, then eat as much as we can and drink as much as we can before climbing them ourselves. I don't know how this is going to go tomorrow, but I do know we might not get much chance to stop for water. We need to be prepared."

I nod, stomach twisting with that well-known fear again.

"Let's go find the stream."

I stand and we carry our weapons through the forest to the stream. Noah places them down by a log and I do the same, then I turn and watch as he takes his shirt and pulls it off, leaving his bare torso on display. My heart hammers, and I wonder for a small moment how the hell I can be looking at him and be feeling attraction when we're in this situation. I guess knowing you could die makes your priorities crystal clear.

My eyes move down Noah's hard body as he shuffles out of his jeans. My heart lodges in my throat as his boxers go next. I can't breathe. He's so beautiful. So perfect. Everything I ever wanted. Strong and dangerous, yet so gentle when he needs to be. His powerful body is sleek and muscled, and I can't tear my eyes away as I move into the stream. No shame. Nothing to fear. He's so strong and so damned incredible. Why did I waste so much time? Why did I let him go?

I move to the stream, trying to calm my pounding heart. I put my back to him and remove my shirt, leaving my bra on. I shuffle out of my jeans next, leaving my panties. Then I lean down and run them through the stream, rubbing them over the smooth rocks to clean them up as best I can. I don't notice Noah coming up behind me until a finger moves down my spine.

I shiver.

"I forgot how beautiful you are."

I swallow and close my eyes, my hands going still in the water.

"Fuck, Lara. You're perfect."

I stand and turn to him, facing a very wet, very naked chest. "Noah," I whisper.

"I would never give that sicko the satisfaction

of seeing me fucking you, but right now that's exactly what I want to be doing. Fucking you."

I tremble and meet his eyes. "Noah . . ."

"Do you remember how fuckin' good it felt?"

I close my eyes. God. Yes. I remember.

I'll never forget.

Noah's lips trail down my stomach, kissing the dip near my pelvis before going lower, his mouth, so hot, sliding down near my sex. I squirm and his big hands close around my thighs, spreading them apart as his mouth moves lower, finding my aching clit. I gasp when his mouth closes over it, sucking deep, long, and hard. I arch, my hips slamming upward, pushing myself closer to his mouth. I want more. God. I want so much more.

"*Noah,*" *I gasp.* "*Please.*"

He flicks my clit with his tongue, driving me wild. I clutch the sheets, toes curling, legs shaking. I need him to fuck me, I need him to keep doing that, I wish he could do it all at once. God, I wish I could have every single thing he's offering in one big hit. My skin prickles as his tongue devours me. He slides a finger down, slipping it between my legs and thrusting inside me. I gasp and cry out his name, pleasure shooting through my nerve endings. "*Noah,*" *I scream, squirming, needing more, needing less, needing to come.*

I need to come.

He fucks me with his fingers, sucks me with his mouth, and my wish is granted. I explode, crying out his name, arching my back. My lips part, my head falls backward, and I shudder until every last twitch of pleasure has been released from my body. Noah has already moved up my body, his big frame towering over mine. He takes my legs and positions them over his shoulders. My favorite position.

"Noah, fuck me," I gasp. "Please."

"I'm about to, baby."

He takes hold of his cock, positioning it at my entrance, then he thrusts. He fills me in one movement, stretching me, filling me. I groan, a mixture of pleasure and pain. He fucks me slowly at first, sliding in and out. I stare up at him through lowered lashes, loving how he looks moving over me, loving how his muscles flex and pull, loving every single thing about him. His jaw is tight as he holds back, but I don't want him to hold back.

"Fuck me like you mean it."

"Dammit," he growls.

Then he fucks me like he means it, thrusting his cock into me, slamming so hard the bed rocks. My legs stretch over his shoulders, my fingers claw the sheets, and I'm coming again before I know it. He keeps driving in and out of me, his powerful body driving his thrusts; our eyes meet and I whimper at how intense he looks right now, staring down at me like I'm the only thing he'll ever want. I think I am. I hope I am.

"Goin' to come, baby," he growls.

"Yes," I gasp. "Yes."

His entire body goes tense and then he's coming, mouth slightly opened, eyes hooded, body tense.

So fucking beautiful.

"I remember," I whisper, cheeks burning as I let the memory slide from my mind. "I could never forget."

Noah looks at me, so intense. I swallow.

He steps forward and cups my jaw, tilting my head back just enough so he can capture my lips with his again. I don't even pretend I can't feel his erection against my belly, hot and hard. I remember exactly how that feels, exactly how well he knows how to use it. I kiss him softly but deeply, taking as much of him as I can get.

He pulls back with a pained groan, pressing a hand against his erection. "I need to cool off or I won't be able to stop."

He turns and walks off, and my eyes drop to his perfect ass as he rounds the corner and heads behind the trees. God. I wish he wasn't so damned beautiful. With one more lingering glance at where he was just standing, I turn back to the stream and finish washing up. I use the water to clean my body, to soothe my sore hands and fingers, then I find a sunny spot to put my clothes to dry.

I sit by the stream in my underwear after that and drink as much water as my stomach can hold. I study my surroundings. If we weren't in the situation we are in, this could possibly be one of the most beautiful places I've been. The trees, the sound of birds overhead, the intense green of the forest, the streams—everything about it is utterly breathtaking.

"How'd you do?" Noah asks, appearing again with his boxers back on.

"I washed as best I could. You?"

"Yeah, same," he says, meeting my eyes for a fleeting moment before hanging his clothes next to mine.

He sits down beside me and we both fall silent.

"What're you thinking about?" I ask him.

"I'm thinking about how tomorrow is going to go. The not knowing gets to me."

"Yeah, me too."

"I don't know what this fucker has planned, I don't know the extent of it. Is he going to come at midnight, in the morning, in the evening? Does he have other traps up his sleeve? What has he planted in this forest? It's all unknown and it terrifies me."

That's the first time I've heard real fear in his voice.

I reach over and take his hand, squeezing it. "Don't give him what he wants, Noah. Don't give him your fear."

He doesn't say anything, but he squeezes my hand to let me know he's heard me.

Now I have to take my own advice.

Late afternoon falls and I find renewed strength as we gather our weapons and some water, get our dried clothes back on, and search for a tree that's easy to climb. I have to believe that we're going to get through this. I have to be strong. I'm in this no matter what I do; being weak is only going to make things worse. For Noah's sake, and my own, I have to dig deep and find something I've fought so hard to bury.

Bravery. Strength. Determination.

I have to be fearless.

Noah finds a tree with some low-lying branches and decides we're going to use it to climb. Once we're up, we're going to move through the treetops as far as we can go; then we'll try to get some rest and just wait. Wait for our lives to be taken into the hands of a man who's capable of anything. We have to trust each other. Pray that we make it out. Pray for a miracle.

"You go up first. Take it easy, feel out the branches."

I look up at the tall tree. I'm terrified of heights, but I'm even more terrified of staying on the ground. I reach for the first branch and use it to pull myself up. That wasn't so hard. I continue on, listening for Noah below me. He calls out, "Don't look down." I wasn't planning to. Branch by branch, we move higher and higher into the tree. I don't know how high the cameras go, but I'd guess not high enough that he couldn't reach them easily.

"That should be enough," Noah calls when I get three-quarters of the way up the tree.

Then I make the mistake of looking down.

It's a lot higher than it felt climbing up. I can't see the ground, just the smaller trees below and their tops. My breath gets trapped in my lungs and all the blood drains from my face. "Look up, Lara," Noah demands.

I can't move.

Oh God. I can't move.

"Lara!"

My legs start shaking, my hands tremble, and I don't think I can hold on anymore. "Noah," I cry out frantically. "Noah!"

"Hang on," he says, climbing faster to reach me. "Don't let go of that branch."

I can't hang on. My hands are losing their grip.

"Noah!" I scream.

He reaches me and wraps himself around me, putting his arms on either side of me and hanging on to the branch. "I've got you. I'm not going to let you fall."

I'm shaking all over, my legs still threatening to collapse beneath me.

"You're okay," he says, his voice shaky, too. "You're okay."

"I d-d-d-don't think I can do this."

"You can."

"I'm scared," I whimper. "I am so tired of being scared."

"Look up at me, baby."

I look up at him.

"You're okay. Say it."

"I'm o-o-o-okay."

"Again."

"I'm okay."

"Again, Lara."

"*I'm okay.*"

"Good girl. I know it's high, but the trees are big and they're sturdy. Hang on and you'll be fine, okay?"

"Okay."

"Do not look down again. Keep your head high."

I nod.

"We have to keep moving, baby."

And we do just that.

They do not get to fuck with my game.

They do not get to kiss.

They do not get to plot against me. Together.

Anger rises in my chest as I run my fingers over the blade of my knife. I need to focus. I've got it all planned. They can't escape. They can work together, but they can't escape.

I imagine this blade driving deep into their bodies, sinking, ripping open their flesh.

I smile as I imagine the sound it'll make. That squelching, bloody sound that makes my skin prickle with anticipation.

Maybe I'll cut their tongues out, or their eyes.

I wonder how well they'll do kissing and giving each other loving glances if they're fucking blind and mute.

Yes.

Imagine that.

ELEVEN

I don't look down again. I follow Noah through the treetops. I don't know how many trees we move across, but for two solid hours we do just that: climb and move. When the sun starts falling, Noah finds a secure tree with a big, thick branch for us to stop on. It's thick enough that I can sit comfortably on it. Fall asleep, though? I doubt it. We can't move through the dark, so now we spend the rest of our night sitting here, wondering what tomorrow is going to bring.

"You okay?" Noah asks, sitting in front of me, legs dangling off either side of the branch.

"Not really, but I don't think I get much choice in that."

He reaches out and takes my hand, running his thumbs over my palms. "I don't know how, but we're going to get out of here, and when we do I'm never letting you go again."

"You're not?"

"Not for a second."

I smile at that thought. Does this mean we're back together? I shake my head. Right now I need to focus on getting out of here, with both of us alive. The rest can wait.

"How do you think he's going to hunt us?" I ask, my voice growing tight with anxiety.

"I don't know. I've thought about it and figure he'd need some sort of transport, maybe something to make him move quicker. He won't do it on foot—at least I don't think he will. I think that's why he's cleared areas and created a rough path. He'd never be able to move through those trees without it."

"So there is a chance we'll hear him coming?"

"I hope so. It'll give us time."

I swallow. There goes that fear again.

"I know it's hard. Trust me, I'm scared as fuck, too, but the reality is that we can't get out of this. It doesn't matter what we do. We have to fight. You have to be prepared for that."

"I am, but it doesn't mean I like it, Noah."

"I get that, baby."

"I'm not going to sleep tonight."

"Me neither," he admits.

"Can we just pretend for the next however many hours that we're not in a tree in a forest being tracked by a killer and that we're just Noah and Lara, hanging out?"

"Yeah, baby," he says. "We can do that."

He shifts around until he's sitting behind me, back to the trunk, arms around me, both our legs hanging. He makes me feel secure like this. He makes me feel safe.

"If you could be eating anything on our tree date, what would it be?" I ask.

He chuckles. "Tree date?"

"That's what we're doing, isn't it?"

"Yeah," he agrees. "I'd be eating pizza."

"Do you still have it with just cheese?"

He laughs and I feel the rumble through my back. It feels good. "Is there any other way to have it?"

"Um, yes. With toppings, like pepperoni and mushrooms and onion . . ."

"Fuck no. That shit ruins it. I don't know who came up with the idea to put all that crap on it, but it should be the way it's intended. Cheese only."

"How boring." I scrunch up my nose.

He snorts. "What about you, little one?" he murmurs into my ear. "What would you eat?"

"You can't guess?"

His fingers find my belly and slip beneath my tee to stroke over my skin. "If nothing has changed then it would be your nanna's apple pie."

My heart aches at the memory of my beautiful nanna. God, I miss her. I miss her so much. Is this my punishment for what happened to her? My heart aches at the thought.

"Stop it," Noah says softly. "Don't let that get into your mind. What happened to your nanna was not your fault, Lara."

"It was and we both know it. I mouthed off and was overconfident. I got myself into trouble and she paid the price."

"You can't do that forever, blaming yourself. She wouldn't want that. You have to let go, Lara. You have to."

"I'm trying," I whisper. "I really am."

"Keep talking. Focusing on that is only going to hurt. Keep talking with me, give me this night with you."

"Okay, Noah," I whisper.

His fingers trail lower, sliding over my hip bones, making it all feel better. The way he always does.

"So we have food for our tree date covered. What else do we need?" I say, voice wavering.

"That a stupid question?" he asks in a husky voice.

"Noah." I laugh softly. "We're in a tree. I don't know how you think that could work."

"I could make it work."

I gasp as his fingers slide beneath my panties to find my aching sex.

"This is wrong," I whimper. "We're probably going to die tomorrow."

"All the more reason for me to touch you once more," he whispers against my ear.

His finger glides down over my clit and he carefully slips one inside. I moan and arch back against him. It feels good. So good.

"You're wet," he murmurs. "Fuck."

"Noah," I half warn, half plead.

"Hush, let me do this."

He moves his hands in that skilled way he has, working my body until I'm on the edge, fingers latched onto his arms, nails gliding along his skin. In and out his fingers pump until I can't take it a second longer. I explode with a cry, my entire body trembling with a much-needed release. Making a pleased, throaty sound, he slides his hand from my panties.

"That was worth every second," he murmurs against my ear.

"What about you?" I whisper into the darkness.

"It isn't about me."

This man. Could he get any better? Why did I deny him for so long?

"Get some rest, Lara."

"I don't want to fall," I admit, even though my eyes are heavy with exhaustion.

"I'll never let you fall, don't you know that by now?"

Yes.

This man.

The sound wakes us.

I don't know it at the time, through the fear and

terror, but that sound is going to haunt me for the rest of my life.

It starts off in the distance, just a low hum that wakes us from our sleep. It takes a moment to wake up and when we do, I realize the sound is getting closer. The sound of a car, maybe a bike. I'm not sure when it's this far away but it's coming closer by the second. My heart jerks to life and I know there will never be another day in my life that I'll wake with this much fear.

There isn't a single word in the world to explain it. It starts at the top of my head and consumes my body right down to my toes. My chest is so tight I can't breathe, my stomach twisting violently and my head spinning. I thought I was strong enough, but hearing that sound coming closer has me questioning everything.

"Noah," I plead.

What I'm pleading for, I don't know.

"Lara," he says, his voice tight and so full of fear it makes my skin prickle.

"He's coming."

He takes a shaky breath. "He's coming."

The sound nears and I realize it's not a car, but definitely a motorbike. Maybe an off-road one. It's traveling slowly, which means he knows where we are. How does he know where we are? We're above the cameras.

"He knows where we are," I say frantically.

"Fuck," Noah curses.

"How does he know where we are?" I yell.

"I don't know, but we have to move. We're high, he won't get a clear shot of us. We have to move, Lara."

He stands, pulling out a spear and a rock from a branch he leaned them against. He tucks the spear into his jeans and clutches the rock in his hand. I do the same, standing on trembling legs. I don't think I can move, let alone climb across trees.

"Move," he barks.

The bike comes closer and my vision blurs as the terror clutches my body. We're going to die. Goddammit. I don't want to die.

"If you see him, don't be afraid to hit him," Noah yells, grabbing a branch and taking himself higher. "Let's get higher."

The bike is right beneath us now, the low rumble like torture to my ears. Tears run down my cheeks as I move higher. Then it stops. It just stops. That scares me even more.

Through the silence, a voice rings out. "You think I can't see you." A male. Familiar. I've heard that voice before. "I can see you. Are you ready to play?"

"Noah," I sob.

"Keep moving, Lara."

"I wonder what I should do to you today," the voice calls. "I don't want the game over too suddenly, and you're making it far too easy for me, climbing those trees. How far do you think you're going to get?"

"Don't answer him," Noah growls. "Move."

"You can only climb so far before you have to come down. Or I can shoot you up there, but that won't be any fun."

I hiccup.

"Scared, are you, Lara? I knew you would be. You're going to be the one I leave alive longer. It'll be fun to watch you beg for your life. I could have picked your friend Rachel for this, but she has sass that girl."

I freeze. Rachel. How does he know about Rachel?

"Did she tell you about our date?"

I shake my head, trying to remember.

"She was so gullible, really. I charmed her socks off and got even more information about you, and the silly girl thought it was because I was into her. Can you imagine?"

I jerk. This man was the one Rachel went on a date with? Oh God. She went on a date with the guy trying to kill us. He got that close? He got that close. I gag. Reality hitting me like a sledgehammer.

"Focus, Lara," Noah calls. "Don't listen."

Tears cause my throat to tighten. My fingers tremble as we climb higher.

"And you, Noah. Thinking you can outsmart me. You can't outsmart me. I've thought of every scenario, including the one you're in right now. Which one of you will I hurt today? Eeny, meeny, miny, moe . . ."

"Noah," I cry.

"Move," he barks. "Now, Lara."

With shaking fingers, I keep moving, climbing higher. The voice below goes silent and trepidation clutches my chest, because that's never a good thing. He's quiet for a reason. That reason is made known in a matter of seconds when an arrow comes shooting through the trees and right past my leg.

"Noah," I scream.

"Move, Lara. Move!"

"I can see you, foolish idiots," he yells from below. "You think I can't, but I can. Stop moving, you're making it too easy."

Stop moving. He's right. Each movement we make has the trees rattling.

"Don't stop moving," Noah says, as if reading my mind.

"If we move, he can see us," I whisper.

"He can see us anyway. Moving gives us a chance."

Laughter from below.

Another arrow comes barreling through the trees, getting lodged in a branch above Noah's head. Bile burns my throat. Noah reaches up and jerks it out, shoving it in his pants. We climb, moving from branch to branch, but those arrows keep coming. Flying through as if there is nothing in their path.

"He's a skilled archer," Noah growls. "He could hit us and kill us, but he's not. He's playing, he's tormenting."

"How can he see us?"

"Just move, Lara."

Another arrow comes up through the small clearing, so close that I'm forced to leap backward. Doing this has me losing my balance. With a terrified scream, I fall. It seems like I'm moving in slow motion, arms flying, legs flailing. I hit a tree branch so hard, I can hear the loud crunch as it snaps beneath me. My screaming becomes agonizing cries as branch by branch, I fall closer to the ground.

To him.

Noah bellows my name, and my hands frantically try to grab onto anything they can. I manage to get hold of a branch on the bottom of the tree, leaving me hanging in the clearing, hands slipping as the weight of my body takes over. It's too thick and I can't get a good enough hold on it. Pain radiates through my body in so many places, I can't pinpoint a single one.

"Well, well, now we're playing for real."

The voice sends shivers running through my body as I look down to see a man wearing a black mask with only two eyeholes showing, pointing an bow and arrow up at me. His voice seems familiar, but I don't have time to think about where I've heard it. I can't see anything else about him, but I don't need to. I need to get the hell out of here, now.

Terror has taken me once more, and I'm frantically trying to hang on to the tree. I need to get back up. My legs flail desperately as I try to pull myself back up onto the branch.

He laughs.

"It's not going to happen, Lara. I'm sorry."

The spring of his wire as he shoots the other arrow is all I can hear in the few seconds it takes to reach me. The tiny device rips through my calf, as easy as a knife through butter. My scream echoes through the forest as I lose my grip and crash to the ground. I don't feel the impact. The only thing I can feel is the agony in my leg, the red-hot, scorching pain that is threatening to take me into darkness.

Through blurred vision, through my screams and hysterical crying, I see him lean over me, that black mask right in my face. Who is he? Goddammit, who is he? "I'm going to give you a head start," he says, evil eyes flashing with joy beneath the mask. "You have two minutes to run, Lara."

What?

I stare at him, pain threatening to cause a blackout.

"Run," he barks.

Run.

Run.

I force my body up, screaming in pain as I start to hobble away down the narrow path. This isn't fast enough. I'll die at this pace. I grit my teeth, suck in my tears, ignore the roaring pain in my calf, and do just what he asked: I run. In the distance I can hear Noah's desperate bellows, but I don't stop. I can't stop. The sound of the bike starting up behind me has me realizing that there is no way I'll outrun this man.

Sick. He's sick.

I run harder, trying to edge off the path, but it's impossible without a giant machete to cut the underbrush. Dammit. I run until I can't breathe, until my whole body is screaming in pain, until my mind threatens once more to shut down. The bike is closer. I can't outrun him. I stop, doubling over with a cry. The arrow protruding from my calf makes my stomach turn.

Weapons.

I straighten and frantically reach into my jeans to pull out the spear that Noah gave me. It's about a foot long with a sharp point on the end. I clutch it in my hands and stand behind a tree, panting as I wait. The bike comes to a stop; leaves crunch as he moves closer to me. "I know where you are, Lara. You're making this way too easy for me. At least show a little fight."

I swallow the vomit rising in my throat.

He gets close enough that I can hear his breathing. I hold my breath and wait as he moves around behind the tree. I clutch the spear. I only get one shot at this. One shot.

"Boo."

He appears so quickly it takes me off guard. I react without thought, driving the spear into his hand that's moving toward me. It slides through his palm easily, far too easily. All the blood drains from my face as I watch red trickle out of the wound. He smiles, and then laughs. Like the pain excites him.

"Is that the best you've got?"

I raise my knee without thought and hit him in the balls. My dad taught me that when I was a little girl, and it's never come in handy until this very moment. He doubles over with a laugh and I take the chance to turn and run. I reach his bike and stop, heart pounding. I have no more weapons. I lost the rock somewhere on my fall. I glance down at the arrow in my leg.

I don't think. I just reach down, take the head sticking out of my calf, and pull it all the way through. I'm already in so much pain, I don't even have it in me to scream. His voice echoes out from behind me and I do the only thing I can. I stab the arrow into his tires over and over, as hard and as fast as I can. Warm blood runs down my leg, but I don't stop. Then with the last bit of strength left in my body, I kick the bike over. I can hear him running toward me. I have seconds, if I'm lucky.

That's enough.

I unscrew the gas tank and watch as the liquid starts pouring out. I don't wait around; I turn and run down the path as quickly as I can. I don't know how much longer I can stay conscious. The pain is too much. It's getting too intense. Laughter fills the quiet space. "Well done, Lara, you're wilder than I thought. You've cut my game short for a few hours. You'll pay for that."

I drop to my knees and crawl into the thick forest off the path, dragging my body through, gasping in pain as I try to get deeper, deep enough that his bike can't find me. Trees block my way, branches tear into my skin, and finally I fall against a log, face pressing against the cold bark. I hear the distant rumble of his bike before finally blacking out.

TWELVE

"Wake up, fuck, Lara. Wake up."

Noah?

I can't move.

"Lara, come on. Open your eyes for me."

I'm trying. I can't.

"Lara?"

Noah.

"Come on, baby, please."

I can hear you. I'm trying.

My body is stiff; I can't move it let alone open my eyes. Noah's voice is fading in and out, and I so desperately want to call out to him, to reach for him, but nothing wants to work. Panic sets in. Am I dead? Is that why I can't move? Worse, am I injured to the point of no return? Is this me dying slowly?

I begin to pant.

"Lara? Hey. Open your eyes. You're okay."

I am?

"Come on, focus."

Focus.

I steady out my breathing and focus. I decide to work on my fingers. A simple task, right? I breathe in and out, then curl my fingers. Noah says something frantically, but I'm too focused on the movement slowly coming back to me. I can feel my fingers! A few more pained breaths and my eyelids flutter open. I see nothing for a few seconds, but eventually Noah's face comes into view.

He looks scared.

"Shit, thank God. You're okay."

I wouldn't go that far.

There is a pain in my leg that's making itself known with every second that my body spends coming back to reality. I groan and try to reach for it, but it seems my body isn't ready for that kind of exertion just yet. Instead I shift, trying to raise it so I can see it. So I can determine what's causing all the pain.

"Take it easy, you've been hurt. Just breathe and let yourself come around."

I focus on Noah. He's got blood on his head. It's dried, but it looks like it dribbled halfway down his face before it got to that point. The sun is beaming through the trees and settling on my thighs, warming me. We're on the path. Did I pass out here?

"What happened?" I croak, my throat dry and scratchy. "You're hurt."

"I just scratched my head getting out of the trees," he murmurs.

"What else?" I ask, rubbing my face.

"You don't remember?"

I close my eyes and focus, trying to get my mind to come back to the here and now. As I do, I remember what happened.

"He . . . oh God."

I push up on my elbows quickly, too quickly. My head spins and I go crashing back down. Noah catches me before I hit the ground. "Whoa. You need to take it easy."

"He was using Rachel to get to us," I cry. "Oh God, how could we be so blind? He was so close."

"I'm sure that wasn't the only thing he was doing, Lara. He probably had many other ways to get into our lives. Now stop squirming."

"My leg," I say through gritted teeth. "How bad?"

"It was a clean wound—you pulled the arrow right through. It's deep, obviously, but through muscle only. I cleaned it up and bandaged it."

"With what?" I ask, my stomach turning violently.

He points and my eyes move down to his shirt, which has been half ripped off. He's wearing the equivalent of a woman's midriff tank. I can't help it, I burst out laughing. It's hysterical, possibly a little crazy, but seeing him sitting there with half a shirt on . . . my traumatized mind finds that hilarious.

"That's funny?" he asks, puzzled.

"No," I say, laughter dying down. "I just . . . I'm sorry. I think I'm losing my mind."

He shakes his head and carefully helps me up, pulling me into sitting position. "How's the pain?"

"It's awful," I admit, trying to ignore the intense throbbing in my calf.

"This isn't going to make things easier. Do you think you can walk on it?"

I shrug. "I don't know. Did he . . ." I look around. "Did he come back?"

"No. You slashed his tires and emptied half his gas tank."

I did, didn't I? I also pissed him off. That probably wasn't a good idea.

"I don't know how I did that. I didn't even think I had it in me, but I was so afraid."

He strokes a piece of hair from my face. "Fear will do that to you. I'm proud of you. Fuck, when you fell from that tree I was sure I was going to lose you, but you were amazing."

"I just did what I had to. You're right, fear does bring out your fighting spirit. I don't want to die, Noah," I say softly, my voice hitching at the very idea that I came so close to it.

"Then we need to see if we can work out this leg. You will die if you can't move."

My heart clenches, but I swallow the worry down and nod. "Let's do it."

He stands first and then reaches for me. His hands curl around my upper arms, and he slowly helps me up. I put pressure on my leg, and while it's painful, it doesn't seem to be a great deal worse than when I was sitting down. "It doesn't seem worse standing."

"Try walking."

I let him go and hobble a few steps. Each time I put pressure on my foot, a pain shoots through my calf—but again, it isn't a great deal worse than the pain that's already there. After a while, I have no doubt it will become more intense, but for right now I think it's tolerable.

"It hurts, but it's not impossible."

He looks skeptical, but nods and says, "I think you should use a stick to take pressure off until . . ."

"Until he chases us again," I finish for him.

He meets my eyes and holds them.

He understands.

"When do you think he's going to come back?"

"I have no fucking idea, and I don't like it. We need to find somewhere to rest, but I don't know if he's going to allow that."

"How long does it take to change a tire?"

He shrugs. "On a motorbike, maybe two hours."

"How long has it been?"

"You've been out cold for about forty minutes."

"So we've got an hour."

He nods. "Probably more, considering he had to get back. Let's go with an hour to be safe."

"So what do we do?"

He looks to the sky, body tense. "We prepare."

Look at him trying to help her.

I shift the ice pack against my balls.

She has more guts than I first thought. I grin at the idea. I wanted her weak, but out there today, chasing her, fighting with her, God, it was incredible.

More than I ever thought it would be.

He couldn't get to her, and that made it even more intense.

She has some fight, the way she ruined my bike. I think I'm going to have fun with her. No, I know I'm going to have fun with her.

I'm going to make her wish she wasn't born, and I'm going to do it slowly.

So comfort away, Noah. It won't matter what you do.

Lara just became my prize.

THIRTEEN

Noah finds a straight stick and re-straps my leg after washing it in the stream. I try not to stare at the small, clean hole, but mostly I try not to worry about the infection that could easily come from a wound like that. There isn't a great deal I can do about it, so I'm trying to take my mind off it. It's hard when the throb is radiating through my body with every step I take.

"You still got weapons?" Noah asks, handing me some water. His eyes are constantly scanning the trees.

"Yeah."

"I don't think going up in the trees is going to work for us again. Even if you were in better shape for climbing, somehow that fucker knew exactly where we were."

I shift on my position on the log, taking a long

drink of water before contemplating what he said. "Yeah," I say. "How do you think he knew that?"

"I'm missing something. I just don't know what it is."

"He's got cameras everywhere. Maybe they're in the trees."

"No," he says, shifting his weight from one foot to the other. "No, he wouldn't have them that high."

"Maybe he's got a few up there, too?"

"Maybe, but it seems far too difficult. I'll work it out. For now we need to figure out what we're going to do the next time he comes."

"Do we hide? Do we run? Do we just fight?"

Noah's jaw tics and he runs a tired hand through his hair. "I don't fuckin' know."

My heart pounds with a familiar feeling of fear and desperation. We both know he's coming back. Neither of us knows when, but it could be any second, or it could be hours. But he is coming back. And he has the ability to find us. He has the ability to hurt us. To make us suffer even more. Any more injuries like the one I received today, and we might not have a good deal of fight left in us.

I rack my brain. There has to be a way to find some sort of safety. I think of everything I've seen out here, but it's all just trees and a stream. A stream. God, how did I miss the stream? Most water supplies come from a bigger body of water. They don't just appear with no source. I stand and shuffle closer to Noah and whisper in his ear, "What about the water?"

"What about it?"

"Well, it has to be coming from somewhere, right? We never followed the stream, but maybe we should. I mean, you'd assume it gets deeper, or maybe will lead us to a waterfall. If we walk through the water instead of outside it, he's going to find it a good deal harder to get hold of us— he's been counting on us not being able to get off the track, but I don't actually think he considered the stream. He'll have to get off his motorbike, and we have a far bigger advantage that way."

He jerks his head back and meets my eyes, then nods. "You have a point, but it may not lead anywhere and we could be wasting our time."

"It's the only part of the forest, outside of his track, that isn't covered so thickly we can't move through it."

"You're right. It's worth the risk to find out."

"Let's go, then."

His breath tickles my ear as he leans in. "It's going to be harder for you to move through the water."

I shrug. "It's that or die, Noah. I don't want to die."

He pulls back and his brows shoot up. "Who are you and what did you do with Lara?"

I give him a weak smile. "Lara doesn't want to die today."

He cups my face in his hands. "Not going to let you die."

My heart pounds and we hold each other's gaze for so long, I'm sure he's going to lean in and kiss me. The air is thick around us and the tension is out of this world. I swallow back the lump in my throat and whisper, "Then let's get moving."

"Let's get moving," he agrees, voice tight.

We fill our coconuts again and shove our spears into our pants. Then we step into the stream and start walking. Noah's right, it's a good deal harder than I first thought it would be, and every step is agony on my leg. But I was also right: The farther downstream we move, the deeper it gets. And as we move in deeper, the stream washes over my wound, numbing it with cold water.

"You okay?" Noah asks after about an hour of silence.

"I can't feel my leg anymore. I think the water numbed it completely."

"Probably not the best idea to keep it so wet," he murmurs.

"No, but what other choice do we have?"

He makes a throaty, angry sound and keeps walking in silence.

We're deeper in the forest now. Trees skirt the edge of the stream and they're cramped together, but stop neatly on the edge, with the occasional few dipping over. We have to push past those, but it's a great deal better than moving on foot down a track created to hunt us.

"This was a good idea," Noah grunts, pushing his big legs through the water. "But fuck, it's hard work."

"You're telling me," I say, voice strained as I force my body to take yet another step.

"Tell me something, distract me from listening for that fuckin' awful noise to come."

"What do you want me to tell you?" I ask, grunting as the water gets even deeper.

"I don't know. Anything. What's your favorite childhood memory? Something I don't already know."

Odd question, but if it distracts me and him for even a second, I'll give it a go.

"My mom got me a puppy when I was five. It was so ugly. I can't even describe how ugly this puppy was. She saved it from a shelter, but it looked like some kind of alien dog. It was skinny with bald patches, with big bulging eyes and an underbite. I loved it, though. I wanted a puppy for so long, I just didn't see how hideous it was until I got old enough to walk it and people used to point on the street."

He chuckles.

I laugh, softly. "Anyway, one day I was walking Pigsy down the street—"

"Wait, Pigsy?" he says, stopping and giving me a horrified look.

I grin. "Yep, Pigsy. I know, it's awful. It seems fitting now that I look back, though. I have no idea how I came up with that name for her."

He keeps walking with a throaty snort.

"Anyway, I was walking her down the street when this old woman stopped me and told me that my dog was quite possibly the ugliest thing she'd ever seen. I was so upset, so devastated. I loved Pigsy. So I told her that if she wants to see an even uglier dog she should look in the mirror."

Noah barks a laugh.

"She grabbed me by the arm and dragged me back to my house, horrified. She told my mom what I'd said and what an awful child I was for being so rude. Do you know what my mom said to her?"

"I'm not sure I want to."

I smile at the memory. "She said, 'My daughter has an eye for beauty, I guess you left yours at home today. You can't blame the girl for calling it like she sees it.'"

Noah chuckles. "God, now I see where you get it from."

"The old woman was so angry, she turned and stormed off. Every time she saw me walking Pigsy after that, she'd turn away and huff, but I'd always wave and greet her."

Noah chuckles. "I miss that side of you."

It feels like a punch in the gut, and I turn to him, whispering, "That side of me got my nanna killed."

"Lara," he says softly.

"That Lara ruined my life."

"That Lara didn't ruin your life. You've gone from one extreme to the other instead of learning to be more balanced. You were such a firecracker and now you're not. You let that Lara disappear completely when you should have kept part of her, because she made you who you are."

As much as he's right—and I know he's right—those words hurt me. Irrationally so.

"What if I'll never be that Lara again?" My voice is soft and a little wounded.

Noah stops walking again and turns, eyes on mine. "You don't need to be that Lara. But you can't be this shell of a person that you've been, either."

I wince. "Ouch."

"I didn't mean it like that."

"Didn't you?" I say, dragging my gaze from his and walking past him.

"Lara," he growls, coming after me. "I didn't mean it like that."

"I think you did. We're in this mess because I'm weak and fragile now and that sicko thought it would be great fun to throw me in the mix because of that. You've made a few comments about how I am. It seems you'd prefer if I was that tough, smart-ass person again. You know I can't be her again. You saw what I went through when Nan died, Noah. I will not lose someone I love again because of that. Nanna warned me, and the least I can do to honor her memory is take her advice and not be that person."

"You're putting words into my mouth," he snaps.

"No, Noah. I'm just putting your words to-gether."

"Bullshit. I fell in love with you because of the way you are. I like this soft, fragile girl that you are now, too. I fell in love with that side of you after Nanna died. But I also liked the little firecracker I met. I hate that you felt you had to be something different. I hate that you think you're not enough, and that I'd sleep with another woman because of it."

I flinch and keep walking.

"Lara," he hisses.

I ignore him because he's right and I'm a damned idiot.

"Lara!"

He barks that one.

I turn to have my say when I hear it. He does, too, because he stops mid-yell and his eyes flash. The motorbike. It's a fair bit away, but the low hum is definitely there.

"Run," Noah barks. "Now."

I don't wait. I start running as fast as I can in the knee-deep water. I give up after about three steps and drop down, using my entire body to glide through the water faster. It's barely deep enough and my stomach drags across the logs and rocks below, but I'd rather this than to face what's coming up behind us.

"Noah?" I call.

"Keep going," he yells.

I do. I just keep going.

The bike is closer now and frustration and fear clash in my chest. Frustration that this man seems to be able find us no matter what we do and fear because he's going to come and I have no idea what's in store.

"The water gets deeper ahead, swim faster."

Noah's right: Up ahead the water darkens and the stream widens. It's getting deeper. Thankfully we chose the right direction to go. If we'd have gone the other way, it would have faded out into nothing. This way is taking us to the source of the water, and we can only pray it's deep and long enough to give us a good escape.

The bike is so close, the loud rumble pierces my ears. Fear makes its way throughout my body and I swim faster, using my legs to push me through the water by kicking off rocks. Noah is beside me, pushing along, too. His big body strains as he tries to glide through the water. Do I look the same? I don't think I've ever swum so hard or fast in my entire life.

"Nice choice, going for the water."

That voice. God, where do I know that voice?

My skin prickles and I make a pained sound in my throat.

"Do not answer, keep swimming," Noah urges.

"I mean, I guess I'd go for the water, too, if I were in your shoes. It'll lead you nowhere, but by all means keep trying."

"Go under the water," Noah hisses through his teeth. "As much as you can. Any weapon is going to have a harder time hitting you under the water. Don't look back for me. Just swim, Lara."

"Where are you going?" I cry frantically when he moves toward the edge.

"I'm going to kill the fucker."

No.

He'll be killed.

"Noah!"

His eyes meet mine and the look in them sends fear right to my core. "Go under, go forward. Don't stop. Don't look back. I will find you, Lara. But don't stop."

"Noah, no," I beg. "He has a gun."

"He won't kill me, not yet. I'm fairly confident of that."

That's a big risk to take.

"He can hurt you. Noah, please . . ."

He stops swimming and comes back over, reaching for me, big hands on my shoulders. "Do you trust me?"

"Yes but—"

He slams his mouth over mine, kissing me hard and fast before pulling back. "Then do as I say."

A tear runs down my cheek, but I nod. I take a deep breath and go under the water just as the sound of a gun firing can be heard through the trees. Pain, panic, and terror mix themselves inside me and I fight against the urge to pass out and vomit, possibly both at the same time. I swim hard and I swim fast, only coming up for air every few seconds. I've always been a good swimmer, doing fairly well at lessons, but this is pushing my limits.

I continue until my entire body is screaming for relief. I have to come up. The water isn't overly deep, but it's deep enough for me to fully immerse myself beneath it.

I skim the surface, lifting just my head out. I can't hear anything. I look around: I'm in a dark area of the forest. The trees are so thick, the sun can't penetrate their thick branches coated with green leaves. The stream has widened into a large creek and I can hear the distinct sounds of a waterfall. Possibly some rapids. I wipe the water from my face with my hands and listen.

Where is Noah? Is he hurt? Worse? I swim to the side of the creek and pull my tired, aching body out. I can barely squeeze through the trees, they're that close together, but I find one with a wide enough gap beside it to sit with my back to the trunk.

And I just keep listening.

I can't hear him.

I can't hear anything.

Oh God, please don't let him be dead.

FOURTEEN

I sit against that tree for what seems like hours. I don't know where Noah is; I don't know if I should go and find him or just wait. My mind is a jumbled mess. If I go after him, I could get lost and might not see him again—or worse, I'll get killed and really make a mess of this. He wants me to trust him so I'll trust that he'll find me. He knows I'm in the water. If he's okay, he'll come find me here. *If* he's okay. My heart twists at the very thought.

Pain lodges itself in my throat and I drop my head in my hands and try to breathe through it.

Losing my leg is a scary reality. Losing Noah is pure torture. I've already lost him once, God. The pain of that will never leave my mind.

I drag my things into Rachel's apartment, face covered with dried tears. I've gotten all my things from Noah's house. I can't be there anymore. The image of him kissing that girl sends agony ripping through my chest. I'll never be able to unsee it. Never be able to live with it. How could he do that to me? I already know how. I let my nan die, I shut down, why the hell would he want to be with me?

But still. I thought . . .

God. I don't know what I thought.

"You okay?" Rachel asks, coming over and wrapping an arm around my shoulder.

"I can't believe he did that, Rach. I . . . I can't get it out of my head."

"Maybe you should talk to him, let him expl—"

"No!" I snap. "No. I won't talk to him. There is nothing he could say that will make this go away, or make it better. We're done. It's over."

"Lara . . ."

"He was kissing another girl, Rach. There is no excuse for that."

"He loves you."

I flinch.

No. He doesn't.

How could he love me? How could anyone love me? No. This is exactly what happens to people like me.

"I've changed my number. If he calls you, do not answer."

I drag my things down the hall, voice devoid of emotion.

"Lara . . ."

I get into my room and slam the door.
This is what I get.

The rumble of a bike has my head snapping up and the memory rushing from my mind. I swipe the tears that have leaked down my face. *No.* There's no way he could have found me already, not that quickly. How the hell is he that good? Where's Noah? Did something happen to him? Panic seizes my chest and I leap to my feet. I don't know where to go or what to do. I look around, frantically trying to come up with a plan as the bike comes closer and closer, torturing me with its sound.

I fumble around, trying to find our makeshift weapons. I can't get hurt again. I don't want to. I just . . . I just *can't.* I don't think I can live through any more pain. I don't think I'm strong enough to fight. I need to escape. That's what I need. The bike speeds through the trees far too effortlessly and I realize the track he created very likely runs the entire length of the stream. Of course it does.

Is that how he's finding us so easily?

"Lara!"

The bellowing sound of Noah's voice has my head jerking to the left.

"Noah?" I scream.

"Run!"

Run? Oh God.

I leap into the water and start moving as fast as I can in the opposite direction of the bike. Logs and rocks tear into the flesh on my legs, but I don't stop. The bike is nearing with every passing second and I know I have no choice but to fight, even though I'm exhausted. Tears run down my cheeks and fear catches hold of my heart for the millionth time in the last few days—but I swallow it down. I suck it back in. I have to fight right now.

"You running is utterly adorable."

The sound of the maniac's voice has my skin prickling. I swim harder, but he appears on the bank before I have the chance to move more than a hundred feet. He's got a gun slung over his shoulder and he's laughing at me, like the idea of me trying to get away is so completely hilarious. I have to fight. Goddammit, I have to fight. I don't know how I'm going to do that. I don't even know where to start. *Find your strength, Lara, or you'll die.* I pull the spear from my pants and clutch it in my hands.

Then I dive under.

I swim downstream as fast as I can, coming up and climbing out of the water. There is a small space beside a few trees, and I tuck myself behind one and just wait. I can hear his boots sloshing through the water as he moves closer. Sweat trickles down my face and my body trembles. I press myself against a tree and just listen.

It feels as if a thousand tiny ants are crawling all over my body as pure, raw terror takes hold.

Fight.

Fight, Lara.

"You have to pay for what you did to my bike,

Lara," he calls, seeming to move closer and closer without even knowing where I am.

How is he doing that?

I stop breathing as he pauses behind the tree I'm hustled behind. I clench my eyes closed, take a deep breath, and then pop them open before leaping around the tree. I pick the right side, see that he has his back to me. I don't hesitate, I propel the spear forward, its point aimed directly at his neck. But before it hits home, he ducks out of the way.

He swings around and then throws his head back and laughs as he turns to face me. He's still wearing the black ski mask, but the evil in his eyes is evident.

"You could have done so much damage with that spear, but I heard you coming and you lost your only chance. You've let me down, Lara."

My entire body shakes as he takes a step forward. He's got a hunting knife as well as the gun, and it's big. I think I'd prefer the bow and arrow.

"Now, I think you need to suffer for what you've done. Don't you?"

I shove the spear out in front of me. "Don't come near me," I yell, voice betraying me by coming out weak and shaky.

He laughs again. "Really, Lara?"

I take a step back. He grins and moves closer. "I think I should remove something from your body, something essential. Say, a finger? What do you think?"

I say nothing. I just lunge. Up close, I see how

big he is, and his body is solid muscle. I'm tiny, haven't worked out in ages, but I have fear and a fierce desire to live on my side. I stab the spear at his heart, but before it makes contact he has my wrist. He bends it back and the spear tumbles from my hand. I'm left with nothing.

Goddamn it.

Laughter fills my ears as he takes hold of my hand, jerking me closer.

"No," I scream. "*No!*"

With a feral laugh, he brings the knife closer. I squirm, thrash, and kick, but he's strong and he's not letting go. I scream and pull as hard as I can, and as if a prayer has been answered, he lets me go. I fall backward, slamming into a tree, my head thrown back to collide with the trunk. Dazed, it takes me a few seconds to gather myself. When I do, I see Noah. He's on the ground, Psycho on top of him, fighting.

God, is that blood?

"Run, Lara," Noah bellows as the knife is raised above his head.

No.

No.

No, Noah.

I don't think, I just charge, bringing the spear under Psycho's neck. Gripping each end and pulling back hard, I choke him while he struggles to escape. For a moment, I think I have him. But he swings around and throws me to the ground, and once again my spear falls from my hand.

I scramble to my feet.

"Run, run, run!" Noah roars, swinging out suddenly and hitting the man in the face so hard he topples back. Then he's charging at me and hauling me over his shoulder.

Noah runs harder and faster than I could have ever imagined a person could, especially with someone over their shoulder, but he moves through the trees on a small cleared track that I realize is yet another creation. He must have followed the psycho in here. He's got blood on him, he's panting, but he doesn't stop. We reach the motorbike, and Noah puts me down.

"Get on," he orders.

I don't hesitate. I just climb on, and in a matter of seconds we're speeding off into the forest, faster than I can handle. I close my eyes, pressing my face to Noah's back. I pray that we didn't escape a killer only to die on a motorcycle. Noah rides for what feels like hours. Eventually, he comes to a stop and looks behind him, eyes scanning the thick shrubbery.

"Without this, he can't catch us. I don't think we'll see him again tonight."

"Are you sure about that?" I whisper, frantically scanning the trees with my eyes. "What if he has another bike?"

"Even if he does, he'll have to go and get it and

we've had a head start. It'll take him some time to catch up."

"I . . . I don't know," I say, my voice trembling.

"We have at least a few hours. He won't come back in without full protection. I can guarantee that. He won't be back tonight."

I climb off the bike and Noah does the same, jerking the key out and tucking it into his pocket.

"This bike might just be our only escape."

He's right about that. It's an advantage—a small one, but one all the same.

"Are you okay?" I whisper, studying him. He has a fair amount of blood on him, and that worries me.

"I don't know," he murmurs, slumping down to the ground, legs out in front of him, big body exhausted. His already torn shirt is covered in blood and has a few extra gashes.

I swallow, trying not to panic at the sight of all his blood. He needs me. He needs me to be strong. I have to get over this. It's just blood. I kneel down beside him and gently start raising his shirt.

"What're you doing?" he says, voice so broken it pains my heart.

"I'm helping. Be quiet and let me work."

He doesn't fight me. He has no fight left. I take his shirt off and recoil at the gash on his chest. It takes me a few minutes to gather myself enough to closer inspect the wound. It's not deep so much as it is long. Thank God. If he needed stitches I honestly don't know what we would have done. I look down at the remains of his shirt, useless to him.

"What happened?" I whisper.

"He got me. Fucker is smart."

I need water. We don't have our coconuts anymore.

I stare down at my still-damp clothes. They'll do.

I remove my shirt. It's still quite heavy with water after my swim. I use it to wipe his body, removing as much blood as I can, then press it over his wound. He doesn't even flinch, he just sits there, staring straight ahead. He's starting to scare me. I keep moving, keeping quiet and working. I wipe his back and move up to his neck, then I stop dead.

"Noah," I whisper, leaning in closer. "What's this?"

He turns slightly. "What?"

"There is something under your skin."

"What?" he demands, reaching up and feeling the small lump sitting just under his skin at his hairline. It's barely noticeable, but now that I'm so close, I can see it quite clearly.

Noah curses and leaps up. "Fucker. Motherfucker."

"What is it?"

"It's a goddamned tracker!"

My heart feels like it stutters to a complete stop. "Pardon?" I croak.

"That's how the piece of fucking shit has been finding us. Goddammit."

I reach up and with trembling fingers feel around my own hairline. Sure enough, I can feel a similar lump. Of course he'd track us. It makes perfect sense.

"How did we not feel this?" I whisper, massaging the tiny device with my fingers.

"They're easily injected. He would have done it when we were drugged."

God.

"What do we do?"

"We get them out."

I know I have a horrified look on my face. Noah walks closer and grabs my shoulders. "Lara, if we don't do this, we're going to keep fighting. We have a solid chance of escaping if the fucker can't find us so easily. He has little tracks and hiding places all through this forest. We've got no hope with these in; without them, we might actually have a chance."

"H-h-h-how are you going to get it out?"

He gives me a pained look. "It's going to hurt, baby."

Tears well in my eyes, but I take a shaky breath and say, "What he's got planned will hurt more. Let's do it."

Noah steps forward and cups my face, running his thumb over my cheek. "Brave, beautiful girl."

My bottom lip trembles.

He leans down and kisses me, long, deep, and full of emotion. I tangle my hands in his hair and kiss him back. I'm done holding back. The harsh reality is that we could die at any minute, and I'm not going to waste any more time pretending I'm not head over heels in love with this man.

"Noah," I murmur against his mouth. "I love you."

He jerks and pulls back, looking down at me. His eyes flash and he says in a low, husky tone, "Don't tell me that now. Tell me when we get out of here."

I give him a wobbly smile.

He just gives me intensity.

I'm okay with that.

FIFTEEN

"This is going to hurt. I'm sorry, baby."

I close my eyes, gritting my teeth and waiting for the pain to come. I know it's coming, I know because I spent the last hour with Noah finding a tool sharp enough to break skin. We found a jagged rock and used another rock to make it even sharper. The very idea of something like that piercing my skin is enough to make my stomach turn.

We found the stream and cleaned it as best we could.

I still don't know if that's enough.

Noah feels around on my neck and I panic, lunging forward. "I don't think . . . I don't think I can."

"Lara, look at me."

He spins me around and his eyes find mine. "If

I don't get this out, he's going to keep finding us and we're going to die. Do you want that?"

"Of course I don't," I snap, then close my eyes. "Sorry."

"Turn around, on three I'll remove it."

My body trembles as I turn and he feels around on my neck again.

"One," he says, voice low.

I clench my eyes closed.

"Two."

He doesn't get to three. A sharp pain pierces the back of my neck and I scream, back arching. A big arm goes around my waist and he hauls me against him, other hand still on my neck. The rock drops to the ground and he squeezes. I try to remain quiet, teeth gritted against the pain. This needs to be done.

"Got it. Hey, it's over. I got it."

He holds me to him, arm still wrapped around me. He presses the shirt I used to clean him up against my neck. It's fresh and cool from the stream. It soothes the throbbing pain. He leans his head on my shoulder and presses a kiss to my cheek. "You're okay. It's all over."

My trembling subsides and I spin around, pressing my head to his chest. He holds me like that for a good long time, big arms closing me in, big body giving me comfort. His hand is still on the back of my neck, and after a while he removes it and gently turns me back and checks the wound. "It's already stopped bleeding."

"Can I . . . can I see it?"

He opens his hand: A tiny, blood-covered device is in his palm. It's no bigger than a grain of rice, and it's gray. Well, I think it's gray. It's hard to tell. Noah's hands are covered in blood.

"Your hands . . ." I squeak.

He wipes them on his jeans. "You've got to get mine out. That prick will figure out we've removed these when he gets back, and it could cause a frenzy. He may head back sooner than expected, so we need to hurry."

That thought terrifies me enough for me to lean down and pick up the rock. I use a new coconut we collected to tip water over it and clean it off. Then I look to Noah. He turns around. I reach into his thick mane of hair and run my hand down until I reach the base of his neck. I find the tiny implant.

"How do I do this?" I ask, fighting the bile rising in my throat.

"You need to get it in your fingers and use the rock to cut the surface. Then you just squeeze."

I swallow thickly and take a deep breath, then I use the rock to slice his skin. He flinches but doesn't make a single sound. I know it hurts—I just had it done—and his strength surprises me. Such a powerful male. Blood immediately pours from the wound and I have to close my eyes and take a few deep breaths to keep myself from passing out. My head spins but I concentrate. He needs me to do this.

I open my eyes and squeeze. The little device pops out and I catch it in my fingers, struggling as I become light-headed from the sight. I press the cool shirt to the wound and turn away. There's so much blood. I close my eyes and try to focus on my breathing. I've already lived through worse than this. I can't let it bother me. No. I'm stronger than this now.

I can do this.

I take a shallow, shaky breath, and then another—until I'm calm again.

After a few minutes, my breathing is strong enough that I straighten and hand him the device. He studies it, then tosses both of them into the stream. He looks up into the trees where he knows the cameras are. "Now the game begins for real."

He's poking the devil.

I can't say I blame him.

"What if there are more?" I ask.

"Come here, we'll check each other."

For the next twenty minutes we run our hands over each other's body, feeling for anything different. The only way we'll truly know if there is another device, though, is to run and see how quickly he finds us.

"What's the plan now?" I ask, staring upward as the sun begins to set.

"We should be fairly safe for the night, and we both need to rest. He'll follow us from the cameras, so we'll have to go up into the trees again."

My heart sinks.

I don't want to climb trees. I want to sleep. To eat. To feel safe.

"I know you don't want to, but we have to."

I know we do.

I nod.

"There are some solid trees up there, good enough to get some rest on. How's your leg?"

"Better than it was."

"Good. Come on, before the sun goes down."

"What about the bike?"

"We could hide it, but if he went through the trouble of putting tracking devices on us, I'm sure the bike's got one, too. Being up there is our only advantage for the moment."

I sigh and we head up the closest, shortest tree. It takes us a solid ten minutes to get to the top, and my leg throbs with every second, but I don't complain. Noah's wounds aren't so bad, and for now, he should be free of infection if we manage to keep clean.

Noah leans into me when we make it onto the second tree. "He can still hear us on the cameras, so don't speak unless you have to. We need to move as quietly as we can or he'll track us by sound."

I nod.

We carefully move through the trees, and honestly, unless he's got superhero hearing, I don't think he'll be able to hear us among the birds fluttering around and the breeze whooshing through. The sun continues to go down, and we move as far as we can without causing too much ruckus.

We make it another hour and a half before we have to stop.

We've skipped through easily forty trees, but in the scheme of things, it's probably not that far. Still, it's the best we've got for right now.

Noah finds a super-thick branch that we can easily sit on, and like last time he presses his back to the trunk and I curl in between his legs, nestling close. He leans down to my ear and whispers, "As soon as the sun comes up, I'm going to inspect one of the cameras. I want to see if I can knock them out."

I turn my head, and he leans down so I can whisper back. "Do you think they're connected?"

"I'm not entirely sure; I need to look at them closer. If I can get to one without him seeing, I might be able to disable some. Throw him off guard."

"How do you mean?"

"It might give us a few hours extra to move away from him if he's busy fixing them."

"The big question here is, How are we going to end this? It's two against one. Surely we have a chance to take him down."

He nods. "Possibly, but today he came so close to being taken out by us. He's not going to be that careless next time. He won't allow us to get that close. I think he's going to up the game."

I swallow.

"You can't hesitate, Lara. If you get close enough to him, kill him. I know that thought terrifies you, but you need to take the chance if it's presented to you."

My body tightens. I've tried to disable him so we could get away. I never considered trying to kill someone before.

"Okay," I whisper. "If that's what it takes."

Noah gives me a soft look before continuing, "I want to try to follow him. I don't know how we're going to do that, but if we can find where he's going back to, we might be able to finish this."

"With those cameras, we'll never be able to follow him."

"That's why they're my next project. They have to be controlled somehow. I'm going to figure out how they work and I'm going to shut them down."

➤➤➤➤◄◄◄◄

No.

No.

Panic takes hold in full force as I study the cameras, watching them remove the trackers from their necks. No. They're ruining my plan. They're changing the rules.

I wipe the blood from my brow, because that stupid behemoth man tackled me. He nearly got me. He nearly ended my game before I even had the chance to play.

Going into the stream was smart. They're smart.

Not smarter than me. I still have my cameras, I'll find them, I'll make them wish they never defied me.

If they're planning on taking me out, they're wrong. I'm going to hurt them so badly, they'll wish they were never born. Then we'll see who has the upper hand.

It's time to kick the game into full force. No more messing around.

They're going to wish they never met me by the time I'm done with them.

Oh wait, no they won't, because they'll be dead.

SIXTEEN

I fall asleep quickly. Noah's arms remain around me all night, and it's good to feel secure for a few hours. We're woken by the sun shining through the branches of the trees. The forest is dead silent, as if everything has just stopped. Or maybe it's just that we can't hear the low hum of a motorbike. Does this mean he hasn't been able to track us?

I can only hope so.

"Morning," Noah whispers into my ear.

"Hey," I whisper back. "He's not here."

"Can only hope that's a good sign."

"Are we getting down from these trees?"

He unwraps his arms from my waist and shakes his head. "As much as I know how nice that would be, we're safer up here until we can figure something out. I'm going to drop down and check out one of those cameras, though. Wait here."

With nothing else to do but wait, I let Noah move out from behind me. Like a thief in the night, he moves silently through the trees until I can't see him anymore. Feeling slightly comforted by the fact that pulling out our chips seems to have worked, I lean back against the trunk and take a few deep breaths.

Minutes go by. Those minutes turn into an hour. Noah isn't back.

I can't call out to him. I don't even know if I should try to find him, but something inside, something right in my very core is telling me to go and look. I stand and leave my things in the tree, trying to take note of everything surrounding it so I'll be able to find my way back. Then I silently move across branches, lowering myself until I can see the ground.

I can't see or hear anything.

I let my eyes scan left and right, then go back up the tree and move along farther, dropping back down again. I do this three times until I finally hear something. It's voices. Noah's, and his. I move faster, gliding through the trees as quickly as I can to get closer to the sound. I reach it and move down through the trees until I can get a picture of the two men. Noah is standing, back against a tree, camera in his hand. The psycho is standing in front of him, gun pointed at his chest.

No.

I go to lunge out of the tree when Noah speaks, stopping me in my tracks.

"You want a real fight? You want a real hunt? Then don't cheat. You claim to be a real hunter, a real killer, yet you're not. You're nothing without those cameras and those chips. You want to play a real game, then play it on even ground."

"I could blow you to pieces right now," the psycho snarls. "And you'd never see the light of day again."

"We both know you're not going to do that, because we both know you want the hunt. You want the game. You breathe for it. You want to make me suffer, to make her suffer."

His body makes a strange shake, and he laughs, low. "I do. I want to hunt you like a pair of fucking rabbits and then skin you alive."

"Then do it, but do it like a real hunter. You want a game"—Noah leans in close, big body strong and powerful—"make it a fair one, because right now you're no hunter, no killer. You're just a cheat. My mother could do a better job."

Psycho stands there, gun pointed to Noah's chest. Then he reaches up and pulls off his mask. I slap a hand over my mouth and gasp as I take him in. Noah barks out a familiar, "You!" But I'm too busy taking him in. The man from the Starbucks. The one who spoke to me that morning. Oh my God. He spoke to me. He acted completely normal. He looks like an average American boy next door. You could walk past him on the street without giving him a second glance except maybe to admire his good looks.

He even told me his name. What was it again? That's right, Bryce.

But as I take him in, I realize that's not the only time I've seen this man.

Flashes of memory run through my head of the night Nan died and . . . oh . . . oh my God. It was him. He was the one who called 911. He was there the moment I lost myself. He was there. All that time he was there. Watching. Waiting. Seeing the change in me. My knees wobble and I have to hang on extra tight to stop myself from falling down. Rachel, my nan, Starbucks . . . he's been there, right in front of me all this time.

I can't believe it. My body trembles with acknowledgment.

"What, nothing to say?" Noah continues, taunting him. "Too weak to play for real?"

Bryce doesn't like that. Not at all. I hold my breath, terrified he'll kill Noah for taunting him, but after a moment he reaches into his pocket and pulls out a device that looks like a small cell phone. He turns it to Noah, and I don't know what's on it, but he raises it up and throws it on the ground. Then he aims the gun and shoots it. I smother a scream with my hand. Heart pounding. Body on high alert. The tiny device explodes.

"Now I can't see you. I can't hear you. I can't find you. That device was the control center for the cameras. Without it, they don't work." Bryce smiles, and it's terrifying. "I'll give you half a day. If I'm going to hunt, I'm going to do it to kill. You think I can't find you without all those cameras, you're wrong. I'll find you, and when I do, I'm going to torture you bit by bit until you're dragging your helpless, broken body along the ground, begging me to let you live. Only then will I end you."

"That'll never happen," Noah snarls.

Bryce laughs. "Oh, but it will."

Bryce steps back, aims the gun, and pulls the trigger.

SEVENTEEN

It takes me a second to realize that he's hit Noah right in the leg. An agonized bellow leaves Noah's throat as he tumbles backward. My hand darts up to my mouth to stop yet another scream. He doesn't know I'm here. *Be. Quiet.* My body trembles as Bryce leans down to Noah and says, "Injury one. Let's see how far you can get now. I'll be back soon, and next time I won't hold back."

Bryce steps back and looks up into the trees. I don't move. I just stay perched behind my branch, praying he can't see me. "Better come and fix your boyfriend, Lara. Now that he's injured, I wonder how well you're going to be able to protect yourself. Oh and by the way, it's lovely to see you again."

He darts around the tree and I see him looking up at me. He grins. Fear clogs my throat.

A second later he turns and gets on his motor-bike, disappearing into the forest.

No.

I wait a few minutes before scrabbling down the tree. Once I near the bottom, I lose my balance. Not wanting to fall on my injured leg, I opt to land on my side. The wind is knocked out of me and I spend a few seconds panting. I clutch my stomach, take a few deep breaths, and then roll and get up. I run toward Noah, who is clutching his leg, face pale, panting. God. No.

"Noah!" I cry, dropping to my knees beside him.

There's so much blood. It's soaking through his jeans, running down his hands. I need to stop it and I need to stop it now. I don't think, I don't even take the chance to freak out. I rip the ban-dage off my own poorly healing wound and wrap it tightly around his leg, trying to stop the blood. "I can't clean it up until the blood is stopped."

He doesn't say anything. He's so pale.

"Noah, hey, look at me."

His eyes find mine, and the pain I see in them makes me want to wrap him up and get him the hell out of this place.

"Hey, you're going to be fine. We're going to stop the blood and clean this up."

He says nothing. He's in so much pain. I can see it. I can hear it in his labored breathing.

I wrap my hands around the bandage and hold firmly. Blood soaks my hands, but I don't care.

The thought of losing Noah far outweighs my fear of gruesome things. I'm not sure how long it's supposed to take for blood to stop flowing, but this seems to be taking longer than I thought it would. I need more pressure. I release my hands, tear off the shredded remains of his shirt, and tie it tightly around his wound.

I pull the fabric as hard as I can to make it even tighter. It takes a few minutes, but this seems to help. I need to figure out how to clean this up, to try to prevent infection. God, what if the bullet is still in there?

His leg is covered in blood. I'm going to need to wash it before I can see anything. The good news is, where the thickest of the blood is, which is where I'm assuming the wound is, seems to have no fresh stuff. Which means we've stopped the bleeding.

"I'm going to rinse all of these in the stream. I need to clean you up."

I stand and gather as many bandages as I can, running toward the stream. I'm thankful for the stream, because without it we'd probably be dead by now. I fall to my knees when I reach it, leg screaming at me to stop, and wash the clothes until the blood has run free and they're as clean as I can get them. I don't wring them out, just carry them back dripping. I need as much water as I can get.

I kneel before Noah when I return, and his beautiful, tortured eyes find mine. "Look at you go," he croaks, his voice so pained it hurts me to hear it. "You're handling this like a pro."

I smile weakly. "I guess he underestimated me, huh?"

"Guess so."

I stare down at his leg again. I take the first soaked item and start wiping. He doesn't make a sound as I clean, but his hands are curled into tight fists beside his body and his jaw is so tight the muscle is bulging out the side. I keep working. I clean away as much blood as I can and then gently place a wet piece of my shirt against his wound. He hisses through his teeth and I look up, feeing awful. "Sorry."

He doesn't speak.

I don't blame him.

I lift it off and study the wound. Thankfully a clean bullet hole.

"I need you to lift your leg. I have to see if the bullet went straight through."

"It did," he grinds out. "Felt it drop when you rolled up my jeans."

God, I know how much that hurts. But it's for the best.

"I don't know if he's hit bone, but it's awfully close to your shin. I can't tell, I can only hope it's just muscle like mine. It'll hurt like hell, but if I can do it, so can you."

I smile pathetically at him. He nods, stiffly.

"I'm going to clean this up as best I can. Then

I'm going to wash these again and dry some out. I'll wrap it up. It's the best I can do."

"Make sure you put one back on your leg. It's bleedin' again."

I glance down and sure enough, my leg is bleeding. I must have upset the wound running around like a crazy person. No matter. "I'll sort it out," I say, reaching for the damp cloth and continuing the cleaning.

Then I go and fetch some more water and squeeze it over his leg, washing the rest away. I do this until it's as clean as I can get it. I lean down, gather our clothes, and once more rush back to the stream. I wash them all again. There is a heap less blood this time.

I hang them up when I reach Noah and hope they dry soon. I don't know how long we've got until Bryce comes back, but we need to find somewhere to hide or we'll get killed. Noah can't run; there is no way he has it in him to fight right now. If we don't get secure, we're going to die, it's that simple.

"We need to find somewhere to hide as soon as I've wrapped your leg."

He looks up at me. "Not fucking hiding."

"Noah . . ."

"That fucker wants a fight, he'll get a fight."

"Noah . . ."

"We've spent most of our time running and look where it's gotten us."

"But your leg is bad, Noah. You need to rest it for as long as you can or you'll be of no use to either of us."

"So you want me to fucking hide while he comes and hunts us down?"

"Yes, actually," I say.

"Well, I'm not doin' it."

"Noah, Jesus!" I yell. "This is not a time to bring your pride into it."

"Pride?" He laughs bitterly. "You think this is about pride?"

"Isn't it?" I growl, crossing my arms.

"No, it's about surviving, Lara."

I shake my head, looking away.

"I'm down, Lara. He shot me down," he says, voice low. "And if I'm not here to protect you . . ." His eyes take on a faraway look.

"Don't talk like that," I warn. "We're going to get through this, but only if we keep fighting. Those clothes should dry out soon. Then we'll go."

"You need to put your pants back on."

"No, they're a good wrap for your leg. I'll survive without them."

"Lara . . ."

"I'm not having this argument, Noah. In the scheme of things, how important are clothes, really?"

His jaw tics.

I say nothing more about it.

"How did you know his name?" I say.

"He came into the station asking for a job a

few months ago. God, I thought he was fuckin' shady back then. Too perfect, you know? There was something phony about him, and the way he was staring at me felt . . . menacing somehow. I should have known."

"He's been here all along. He was the man who called nine-one-one the night Nan died, he went out with Rachel, and I remember him speaking to me in Starbucks one morning. He's just been here all along, watching us without us even knowing."

Noah looks angry, perhaps mostly that some one could have been so close to us all that time without us realizing.

"I should have known," he growls.

"It isn't as if he said anything threatening, Noah. Neither of us knew."

I find a tree and sit down, leaning against it, trying to ignore the pain in my own leg. Last night we were so sure we had the upper hand. Now we just have to figure out a way to keep it.

We have to.

We will.

EIGHTEEN

When the clothes are dry, I secure Noah's leg as best I can. Then I re-cover mine after gently washing it. It's a little red and inflamed, but I pray that's only because I just ran around in the forest and irritated it. I can't deal with infection right now. I help Noah to his feet, and his body stiffens in pain after the first step.

"Come on," I say as he takes another step. "There has to be somewhere we can find that's hidden and secure."

"Won't matter. That fucker will know every hidey-hole in this place. Every spot that's cleared, every track, everything is made by him. Even without those cameras, he knows we can't get far off these created tracks, so he'll find us eventually without looking too hard. He knows it. I know it."

"Yes, he might, but he can't look everywhere at once."

"He'll look in the ones closest to the area he shot me. He's not stupid, Lara. He knows we can't get far."

But we can.

"I have an idea. It's not the best for our legs, considering all the work I just did, but I think it'll work."

Noah glances at me, face tight.

"Trust me," I say, taking his hand and carefully leading him to the stream.

"Get in," I say, pointing to it. "I'm going to do something."

"What?"

"I'm going to run along in the opposite direction and put a couple of things down, just subtle things. It might lead him off in the wrong direction and give us time."

Noah's face flashes with a look of indecision before he stiffly nods.

"I'll be back soon. Sit by the stream and don't move."

I gather a couple of small scraps of material and a coconut. Then I turn and jog as best I can into the forest. I find where Noah was sitting and use some of the cloth to soak up the blood all over the ground. God, there was a lot of it. I stomp my feet in it, cringing, and then start walking in the opposite direction to the stream. I leave a few bloodied footprints, mark a few leaves on trees with blood, leave a strand or two of cloth fibers on sticks. I even break a few branches.

It takes me well over an hour to complete this, and then I have to very carefully come back, stepping as close to the edge of the track as I can, making sure I cover every one of my new footprints so he doesn't figure out what I've done. It takes me a good long while to get back to Noah, and when I get there, I find him slumped against a tree, head dropped, eyes closed.

I run forward. Fear clogging my throat.

"Noah!" I scream, dropping to my knees in front of him.

I take his shoulders and shake, panic gripping my chest. No.

His eyes flutter open. I make a strangled, relieved noise.

"I was just resting, Lara," he croaks.

Tears burst forth; I have zero control over them. They tumble down my cheeks in rivers. "I thought . . . for a second I thought . . ."

He reaches up, gripping my chin. "I'm okay. I'll be okay."

I nod, sniffling, trying to suck back my sobs. Noah's fingers move to my jaw and then glide up until he's cupping my face. "Hey, where's that brave girl who just told me we'd get through this if we keep fighting?"

I nod fiercely, wiping away my tears. "You just

scared me for a minute, that's all. The thought of losing you—"

"You won't. Do you hear me?"

I glance down at his bloody leg.

No.

Not yet.

"We should go," I say, standing. Feeling his hand drop away from my face hurts, but we don't have time to do this. Not right now.

"Yeah," he mutters, standing with a wince.

We step into the stream.

"Where did this end up?" he asks, as we slowly start following it down.

"It ended up in a big dam-like thing, but the forest around it was really thick and dense. He has tracks running alongside it, but if we're in the water he'll be forced to get off his bike and come in. I think if we go farther than I went, it'll get even denser. It's hard to track someone through water, and soon it'll be deep enough that we can take the pressure off our legs and swim as best we can."

"Anyone ever tell you that you're an incredibly strong, brave, and fucking beautiful woman?"

I flush and look to him. "Yeah."

"When?" he frowns.

"Just now."

A grin.

He's going to be okay.

We're okay.

For now.

Not a real hunter.

How dare he.

I'm a real hunter. I'm better than anyone. It took me ten years to create every track, to clear every clearing, to plant trees, to keep the stream clear enough to flow. I thought about every scenario, every escape.

Not a real hunter.

He has no idea who he's challenging. I'll find him without those cameras and those damned chips.

I'll make him wish he never challenged me.

I know every inch of this forest.

Every. Single. Inch.

They won't escape me.

Tomorrow, I hunt.

And this time I shoot to kill.

NINETEEN

Agony.

It comes in so many forms. Physical. Mental. Emotional.

I'm feeling all three.

I don't know how many hours we've waded through the water, but my mind, my body, my soul are shutting down. Everything hurts, inside and out. My tired body just doesn't want to take anymore. Noah is the same, I'm sure of it. Nothing takes the pressure away. We've floated, we've swum, we've just stopped and lain down. Nothing is taking the pain away.

It's the afternoon now, that much I know. The sun has changed directions in the sky. Isn't it funny how we notice these things? You can go through your entire life not noticing the simplicity of the earth, yet when it's all you've got, suddenly it's black and white. The sun. The trees. The weather. The way the animals move. The way the days pass by. It's all so clear, creating its own pattern. We as humans choose not to see these things, but when you stop and look, it truly is beautiful.

"Lara?"

I turn toward Noah, who is staring straight ahead.

"Yeah?" I croak, voice tired.

"Look ahead."

I glance ahead and stop dragging my legs through the water. Directly ahead is a waterfall. It's not big, but it's a decent size. Rocks climb either side of it, stretching up and then continuing on toward what I assume is more forest.

"It's a waterfall," I mumble.

"Most waterfalls have little nooks behind them."

"Where do you get that logic?"

He shrugs. "It's always in the movies."

"And everyone knows the movies are based on fact."

He gives me a look.

I give him a sheepish smile. "Sorry, I'm starving and I'm tired."

"Let me go ahead and check it out."

"No," I say quickly. "Your leg is numb from the cold water, but I can tell you now that it's going to hurt like hell when you get out of here. Let me check it out."

He glares at me. "Yeah, that's not going to happen."

"Noah."

"Lara."

I sigh.

"Stay here," he mutters and uses his arms to swim his body across the deep dam leading up to the waterfall.

He reaches it and I watch as he uses his powerful body to haul himself up. I can see the pain on his face, even from here, but he doesn't make a single sound. He just climbs in, shoving through the water. I float, and I wait. Five minutes later, he comes back out. He's got a relieved smile on his face. That must be a good sign, right?

"What do you know, the movies are right," he yells.

Thank God. I swim over, using the last of my energy. I reach the waterfall, and the soft mist created from the water crashing down over the rocks soaks my face. I close my eyes and reach for the hand Noah extends. He hauls me up as if I weigh nothing and I have to hold my breath as we shove through the waterfall.

We get blasted with water from every angle. It pounds down over our heads, nearly taking my feet out from beneath me. I keep holding my breath and hanging on to Noah's hand as he pulls. Step by step we go. My lungs feel like they're going to explode. Finally, the water stops. I open my eyes and blink a few times, clearing the water from them.

"Wow," I breathe.

"Yeah," Noah mumbles, walking in and running a hand through his hair, flicking water everywhere.

"This is . . . *magical*."

I take in the small but cozy space in front of me. It's cave-like in its creation, with high moss-covered rock walls. The only difference is that the area to the left has a small opening in the rocks, perhaps from damage, and a little natural light is flowing in, lighting up the space enough to see where you're going. Water is trickling down the walls in tiny streams and I can hear the water roaring overhead. I can also hear it in the cave, but where it's coming from I don't know.

Noah hobbles around, examining the space inch by inch. "Check this out," he says, encouraging me over with a hand.

I limp over and peer in. He's pointing into a deeper part of the cave, which to be honest looks like it might continue for a good long while. "How far do you think this thing goes?" I ask, squinting into the darkness.

"Could go for miles. No way to tell. It might be tiny, it might be never ending."

"Do you think he knows about it?"

"Well, we've gone off his track, which makes me wonder. The only way we'll know is if he shows up. But to be honest, this cave looks untouched. Getting in here was a big effort and it wasn't easily visible from the outside."

"Do you think he's even ventured this far into the stream?"

"No way to tell, but given how far off the track we are, my guess is that we're in one of his blind spots. We just might have found a safe place."

Hope explodes in my chest, but I do my very best not to cling to it. Knowing we had a safe space . . . that would mean everything.

"Should we go deeper?"

He looks into the darkness for a few minutes, then turns back to me. "At this stage, no. There isn't light in there, and it could be dangerous. We didn't come this far to fall and die."

"Well," I say. "I'm happy to have a safe place for now."

"Don't know that it is one yet, but I'm hangin' on to hope."

"Me too," I admit.

"We need to get dry and we need to air out our wounds. Do you have any objection to getting naked so I can dry out these clothes?"

I blink. "Was that a pickup line or . . ."

He grins. "Jesus, woman. No. It's survival."

"Sure it is," I mutter.

"Okay, well, sit in wet clothes."

"I have underwear," I point out. "I'll sit in that."

He shakes his head and removes everything he's

still wearing, down to his boxers. He unwraps his leg and I can clearly see the wound now. It's so clean from the water. It's just a big, gaping hole. The gash on his chest is so clean I can hardly see it, but it's there, skin peeling on either side of it. I turn away, finding it painful to look at. I unwrap my own leg, strip down to my underwear, and hand Noah my clothes.

"I'm going to see if I can find a way to get out and put these in the sun without going through the water."

I nod, pressing my back against a cool rock. My eyes are heavy and my body is exhausted. Hunger growls low in my belly and I'm thirsty, even though I just spent hours in water. I shuffle forward, moving toward the natural light shining in. The sun is blaring through and I sit directly beneath it, feeling its warmth against my skin and sighing with bliss.

"Sorry to burst your bubble," Noah says, stopping in front of me. "That's the only sunlight."

I want to scream and rip my own eyes out, but instead I shuffle back and let him lay out the clothes. "Do you think we'll have enough daylight left to dry those?"

He shrugs. "Don't know, but I hope so. How's your leg?"

I stretch it out in front of me, and it throbs. "Killing me," I admit. "Yours?"

"Same," he mutters, sitting down beside me.

It's warmer here, so even though I'm not directly in the sun, I decide to stay as close to it as I can get.

I sigh and drop my head into my hands. My hair falls down over them; it's a tangled mess, strands matted together to form dreadlock-type creations. Noah reaches over, wrapping an arm around my shoulder and pulling me closer. "You hungry?"

I nod.

"I saw some wild plums growing near the waterfall," he says. "I can go get some."

"In a minute," I murmur, turning and pressing my face into his chest. He's warm, and he smells familiar, which I need right now more than anything. A familiar comfort.

He hangs on to me, fingers combing through my hair as best they can. We don't move, we just sit like that for what seems like ages, in each other's arms, taking the only comfort we have right now.

"Let's eat, drink, and get some rest while we can. We'll take it in turns. You sleep, I'll keep a watch, then vice versa."

"Okay," I say, voice weak and tired.

"Okay, baby."

He lets me go and I immediately miss his warmth. He goes back outside and soon returns with his hands filled with wild plums. He's beside me again, handing one to me. I take it and eat it, then finish another. Then we drink from the stream.

"Sleep, honey," he murmurs, looking down at me. "I've got us covered."

I don't argue.

I don't believe I have the strength.

I just lie down on the warm rock and let my eyes flutter closed.

For a few hours, I pray I'll find peace.

TWENTY

I wake to hands running over my cheeks and Noah's quiet voice. "Lara?"

I shift, back aching from lying on the rock. It takes me a few minutes to open my eyes, and when I do it's still fairly light in the cave. I'm guessing it's late afternoon. I mustn't have slept long.

"What is it?" I whisper, groaning as I shift.

"He's out there."

My entire body freezes. Three words. Isn't it funny how they can have that effect on you? In a split second I go from relaxed to utterly terrified. I'm tired of fear. Tired of living with it constantly weighing down on my chest.

"What?" I whisper, throat tight.

"I heard the bike about five minutes ago. It's stopped."

"Do you think he knows we're in here? Oh

God, Noah. We can't get out. This was a stupid, stupid idea and—"

"Hey," Noah growls low as he kneels down. "We don't know anything. Just be quiet. Don't move. Don't make a sound."

I look toward the waterfall that pounds over the opening to our little cave. I can hear the distinct sounds of someone moving near the water, possibly even in the water. My entire body goes stiff as the sudden onslaught of a flashlight moves across the waterfall, seeming to hang there for too long. I close my eyes, hold my breath, and for a few torturous seconds I honestly cannot feel anything but pure, raw terror.

From the top of my head right down to my toes, everything tingles. Every part of my body feels as though it's going to explode, and I want it to. I never want to feel so utterly petrified again in my life. I can't manage a breath, even as I try. I just sit there in Noah's arms, eyes clamped shut, praying, just praying that someone up there can hear me. *Please don't let him find us in here.*

What seems like hours pass, but in reality it's only a couple of minutes. The sound of the bike starting up has my body jerking in Noah's arms. My eyes dart open and I listen as it zips away. Just like that. Gone. Noah and I don't move for a solid five minutes, just sit there, tense, waiting to see if it's some sort of trick.

But he doesn't come back.

"He doesn't know we're in here," Noah says, voice thick.

I cry silently.

It seems fitting. Relief unlike any I've ever felt in my entire life washes through me and I slump into Noah's arms, wrapping myself around him, pressing my cheek to his chest.

"We have a safe place," I whisper against his skin.

"For now we do."

"For now?" I ask, lifting my head and looking up at him.

"If he doesn't find us in a few days, he's going to get desperate. Probably turn the cameras back on. And I'm not sure we have that kind of time anyway. We can't go that much longer without medical attention."

There goes that relief.

It slides out of my body as if it were never there.

"So what do we do?"

"We stay in here as long as we can, make weapons, come up with a plan. We have to end him. It's the only way we'll get out of here."

"So ultimately, we're going to play his game."

Noah looks at me, his face hard. "He'll find us, eventually. We can't hide here forever. To end this, we have to face him."

"We tried that before, Noah," I say softly. "We're no match for him without real weapons."

"You don't need weapons to take someone

down, you just need the right plan. He's one person. We're two."

"One person with a plan and weapons."

"Are you saying we should just give up then?" he says with frustration.

"No, not at all. Just that we need to be careful. If we go rushing in, all this has been for nothing."

"I know," he says softly.

"I don't want to die," I whimper.

His hands go to either side of my head and he leans in close. "You're not going to."

"I want to live."

"You will."

"I want," My voice cracks. "To love. To kiss. To make love. I don't want all those things to be taken from me. I want them. I need them. I want them all just once more."

He leans down, breath fanning over my face. "You'll have them more than once more. You'll have them for the rest of your life. We're going to get out of here, Lara."

"You can't promise that."

His eyes scan my face. "I'm not going to give up."

A tear runs down my cheek. He captures it with his thumb.

"But if there is a chance we don't make it out," he says, voice husky, "then I'm going to give you all your once-mores."

My heart pounds.

"Starting with love."

I swallow the thick lump in my throat.

"I love you, Lara. Loved you from the second I laid eyes on you in that bar. I've loved you every minute since."

More tears.

He leans in closer, kissing them away. Then his lips find mine and he kisses me softly at first, moving his lips over mine, coaxing me. A few seconds of gentle, loving kisses continue until I finally part my lips and let him in. His tongue finds mine in a gentle caress that I feel right down to my toes. I reach up, curling my fingers into his hair, pulling him closer, molding our bodies together.

The kiss blows my mind.

"A once-more kiss," he murmurs against my mouth before pulling back.

My stomach does a tumble and my heart flutters.

"Now, for the last one. What was it?" he rasps.

His finger trails over my bare shoulder, causing my skin to prickle. He runs a hand down my arm, capturing my elbow and bringing me so close I can feel every hard inch of him pressing against me. I tremble in his arms and look up at him. "I want you," I breathe. "I need you."

He reaches up and captures my jaw, tilting my head back. "Who am I to say no to your needs?"

I smile.

He grins.

Then his lips find mine again. This kiss is rougher, more passionate. This is the way I remember him. Wild, feral, so damned masculine. His hand slides down and captures my ass, using it to grind my body against his. I don't feel the pain in my leg, or my tired body; all I sense is him. All around me. Taking away everything else for just a minute. Our tongues dance as his hands move over my body, stroking, kneading, giving me what I so desperately need.

His hands make light work of what remains of my clothes, and with a bit of shuffling we manage to get him naked, just enough. We only need just enough. Our mouths clash in a frenzy and we suddenly go from soft and gentle to desperate and needy. My nails graze his biceps, tearing into his skin, making him hiss. His fingers knead my ass as he grinds me against his erection. I'm wet. I'm not ashamed. I mewl against him, needing him, wanting him. Right now.

His mouth tears away from mine and drops down, capturing a nipple between his lips. I arch with a gasp, hooking my good leg around his hip and using my heel against his back to drive him closer. His erection glides up and down my sex and we both let out a feral groan. He nips my hardened nipple and moves to the other one, licking and sucking until I'm writhing against him.

His hand moves between us. He takes his erection. Then he's inside me. Months without him, all the tears I've cried, it all washes away as he drives upward, filling me in one, swift movement. It feels incredible. So fucking amazing. I cry out his name as he stretches me, causing a slight burn to mix with the pleasure. The right kind of mix. The perfect blend. I clutch his shoulders, ignoring the pain in my body, focusing instead on the incredible pleasure going on between my legs.

"Noah," I whimper against his neck. "Oh God."

"I forgot how good you felt," he growls, thrusting into me, his powerful body holding me up with little to no effort.

"I'm going to—"

I throw my head back and it bumps against the cave wall behind me. I cry out his name as an orgasm rips through me, hard and fast. My entire body shakes with pleasure as his thrusts become quicker, until he's driving in and out of me. Holding me up couldn't be easy. A few thrusts later, he explodes, gasping my name and dropping his forehead against mine. A fine layer of sweat covers his skin, and we're both panting.

"Well," I say, voice breathy. "If that's my last time, it was totally worth it."

He chuckles and gently releases me.

"Are you okay?" I ask when my feet hit the ground.

"Better than okay."

"I mean your leg." I smile wryly.

He runs a hand through his hair, and I can't help but notice his biceps and how they flex as he moves. God he's perfect.

"It's fuckin' killing me."

My smile dies. "Then we shouldn't have—"

He cuts me off with a kiss, rough and quick. "I'd do that to you given the chance even if I was missing a damned leg. I've missed you so fucking much, Lara. Being away from you killed me."

My heart hammers. "I'm sorry. I've missed you, too."

He grins.

"I don't know how long we've got, but I think we can safely say we've got the rest of the night. Let's get some sleep. We both need it."

"First let me look at your leg. I want to make sure it's okay."

He gives me a look.

"What?" I protest. "I don't want it to actually drop off."

He finds a spot and lies down. I get to work on checking his leg. It's still fairly clean and oozing a little. It could be worse, but he was right earlier. It desperately needs medical attention. He's not going to last the next few days. I go over to the waterfall and dip a shred of what's left of his shirt into the water before moving back and gently cleaning off his wound. Then I find a small rock and raise his leg a little, hoping it'll take some of the pressure off and he'll manage some sleep.

"I don't have anything to take the pain away, but I hope you're tired enough that you manage to get some rest even through it's probably killing you."

He smiles weakly. "I think I'm tired enough."

I take some of the dry clothes and roll them up, tucking them under his head. Then I lie down beside him. He pulls me into his arms and I throw mine over his stomach, nestling into his chest.

In a matter of seconds, we're both asleep.

TWENTY-ONE

Noah is in agony.

There is no denying it. He winces when he moves, he woke up numerous times groaning in pain, and he's got a constant sweat shimmering on his skin. He's suffering with a pain I can't fix. I hate knowing I can't help him, that no matter what I do I can't take it away. We've been in this cave an entire day, and while we haven't been found, we're going to have to leave soon to get food. We're both hungry. Noah is in no state to do that right now, and that leaves only one option.

I have to do it alone.

The idea of going out there by myself terrifies me, but I don't let it show. I'm trying to be strong. He needs me to be strong. He's been my rock, a tower of strength, but he needs a little more time to rest and I need more plums so we can eat while we have a chance. So I've made the choice to go when he falls asleep next. He won't let me go otherwise. He's outright refusing.

"How's the pain?" I ask, kneeling next to him.

"It's a little better," he says through clenched teeth. "But not much."

"You need to rest, Noah. If you don't, we'll never get out of here."

He looks up at me, and the pain in his eyes hurts me to see. It fucking hurts.

"I know," he rasps.

"I'm going to rinse one of these cloths and put some water on it. The cold might help relieve the pain."

He says nothing, just closes his eyes. I walk over to the waterfall and run part of his shirt underneath it, then carry it back and press it over his wound. He sighs, with relief or pain, I don't know. I've been doing this on my own wound and it's been helping. I have no idea if it's useful or not, but the cold seems to take away the pain for a few seconds. We both likely needed stitches, so our wounds are healing wrong, but there is little we can do about it.

Noah's breathing deepens after a few minutes and I sit back, just watching him. He made me promise I wouldn't go out of this cave without him, but I need more food. The water will help and we both need to eat. If we're going to get our strength up we need to eat, pure and simple. He's not going to be happy with me, but I'll be in and out so fast, he'll probably never know.

I wait another ten minutes, until I'm sure he's asleep, then dress in only my bra and panties, because those are the only clothes left in one piece, and head toward the waterfall. I reach it, take a deep breath, and start shoving through. Just as when I came in, my lungs scream and my body begs for air as I push my way out. I reach the edge and topple downward, not realizing I was so close. It isn't a high ledge, but it's enough that I hit the water with a fair amount of force and a loud splash.

I surface, gasping for air, eyes darting around to make sure Noah didn't hear me—and mostly to make sure I'm alone. I wait a few minutes, and nothing happens. My heart pounds as I swim to the side of the dam and climb out. I look left, then right, and decide on going back the way we came. I know the plums must be that way.

I find one of the created paths leading to the water after I've swum for about fifteen minutes. I climb out and move down it until I find the plums. Panting, I hunch over and catch my breath. It was hard work swimming that fast, but I need to be quick. My leg throbs and my head is a little light from lack of food. I study the trees.

I peer up at the shortest of the four trees, which seems to have the most fruit.

I reach for one and pluck it from its branch.

"Hello, Lara."

That voice sends chills right up my spine. I turn slowly, plum in hand, to see Bryce stepping out from behind a cluster of trees. My heart launches into my throat and I can't breathe. For a few seconds I just stand there, unable to move.

"H-h-h-how did you find me?" I gasp.

A stupid question, but it gives me a chance to think.

"The plums you found were strategically placed. There's only so much food out here, and I knew you'd have to find some soon, and I took a guess that you'd be near the stream. I saw your attempt at throwing me off guard, by the way. It was pathetic. I knew you'd go in the water, it's rule number one of survival when you don't want to be tracked. I figured you'd end up around this area and I was right. And your boyfriend said I couldn't hunt." He throws his head back and laughs. I stare at the weapon in his hands. It's a knife, a big, big knife. I swallow. "How is Noah, by the way?"

"Go to hell."

"Is that really the best you've got? I thought better of you, Lara."

"Go to hell, Bryce."

"All that time, I was right there and you never knew. I even set up Marco to buy you some drinks and drug you. Naive idiot did whatever I asked for the right price."

Marco? Is Marco the guy Noah saw me with? God. Where does it end?

"And you just ate that up so easily. A little attention and you were putty in his hands."

"You're a monster," I whisper, trembling.

He laughs. "I never claimed I wasn't, but you, my dear, are gullible."

I spot a large rock, grab it, and throw it at him.

It's the only thing I can think to do and it takes him by surprise, catching him in the head.

He takes a few wobbly steps backward but I don't wait to see if he manages to stay on his feet or not. I turn and run. I run hard, I run fast, I run fueled by fear.

Wild laughter follows me.

"You can run, but you can't hide."

I can hear his boots pounding after me.

Tears run down my face as I pick up the pace. I can't go back to the cave; I have to try to hide. If he can't track me, he can't find me. I push past leaves and trees as they grow thicker. I stumble over rocks, but I don't stop. Sweat runs down my forehead and adrenaline spikes, causing me to pick up the pace even further.

I turn and look behind me—a huge mistake. I slam into a tree, sending my whole body launching backward. I land on the ground with a thump and a strangled cry. I flip my body over as quickly as I can and start frantically crawling toward the thickest parts of the forest, off the track. I'll risk whatever's in there if I can hide.

It's not enough.

He comes out of nowhere, as if he wasn't even trying. He reaches down, hooking a hand around my ankle.

I scream.

As loud as I can.

Then I kick backward, hitting something, I don't know what. I keep doing that, kicking over and over as I try to free my ankle.

"I could kill you so easily, but I made a promise. I said I'd injure you, little by little. If you'll just stay still, I can make it quick."

"Fuck you!" I spit, flipping myself over and driving my foot into his face.

He topples backward and I leap up, spinning to run again. He throws the knife, like some sort of goddamned pro. It hurtles toward me and hits my arm, its blade slicing through my skin as simply as if it were gliding through butter. Stars cloud my vision as pain rips through my body. Blood comes gushing out, running down and dripping over my fingers.

Run, Lara.

Run.

I force my legs to move; somehow I force them to go even though everything inside me wants to curl up and die. I grip my arm, blood flowing over my fingers, and charge down the track. Laughter follows me, along with footsteps. He won't get me again. He won't. I have to hide. I run faster, so fast my lungs burn and my breathing practically stops.

Sweat burns my eyes, but I don't stop. I don't

let go of my arm. I think of Noah. I think of freedom. I have to get through this. I have to. I don't know at what point I lose him, I just know that his footsteps seem to quiet behind me. I run and run until my body refuses to take anymore. I stop for a split second and glance around. The forest is thick, deep, dense on both sides of me. Exactly what I need. I won't get far in there, it's so cluttered, but I'm willing to try.

I can't run any longer.

I step off the track and shove in between two massive trees. Vines swing, crisscrossing over them, and I have to use the last of my strength to push them up. Bushes and logs are so thick, so cluttered that I can barely move two steps without having to haul something out of the way—Noah was right, we never would have been able to navigate through here. Still, I keep going until I'm about two yards in.

I spy a thick bush and, exhausted, press myself into it as deep as I can. Branches scratch my arms and tangle in my hair, but I squat down, drop my head, and try to steady my breathing. A few minutes later, I hear his footsteps fill my quiet space. I got farther ahead of him than I thought. I close my eyes, clench them actually, and wait. He's walking slowly, almost silently.

I hold my breath.

There isn't much left to hold, but I'm not going to let it out.

"Lara?" he calls, his voice almost melodic in its

sound. "Come out come out wherever you are. We're not done playing."

I don't move.

"Noah was right about the cameras, this is so much more fun."

Don't. Move.

"You know, if you want to play, I'm great at hide-and-seek."

Bile rises in my throat.

"Oh Lara."

I pray the bushes surrounding me are enough, that he won't be able to see me inside them. I stay crouched like that, listening to him tormenting me for what seems like hours. Slowly but surely, his footsteps move off in a different direction and fade away. I still don't move. I stay crouched, breathing so softly I wonder if it's even enough, for so long my body screams at me to move. My muscles cramp, my back aches, and my legs throb.

But my arm.

The agony is almost unbearable. I'm bleeding so much.

I finally decide to move and slowly shuffle out of the bush. I wait to see if he'll just leap out, but he doesn't. I don't know how far he's gone, or where he'll be waiting, but I know the game just went from bad to worse. He's hunting now, for real, and I don't know how the hell we're going to beat him.

I stand there, in the middle of those bushes, for another ten or so minutes, just staring, waiting, not trusting that I'm alone. It becomes clear after a while that I am, and I shuffle out with great difficulty. When I'm back on the path, I lean over and gag, my stomach empty but still wanting to purge itself. It hurts. It all just hurts. Noah was right, I shouldn't have come out here, but I did and now I'm paying for it.

I don't even know where I am.

I don't know which way I ran.

I don't know how to get back to Noah, I don't even know if he's okay.

I just know I'm alone.

So utterly alone. And I'm terrified.

TWENTY-TWO

The pain is too much.

I walk in the direction I think the cave lies in, but the fact of the matter is I could be completely wrong. It all looks so similar. It could be the wrong move, I know that, going back to the place I was hiding because he may be there, lying in wait, but I don't want to get lost in this forest, because I'd lose Noah, and we're stronger as a team. At least the bleeding from the gash in my arm has stopped. It's not as deep as I first thought, but I've no doubt doctors would have a serious discussion about stitches if I were at a hospital.

I start moving, slowly, cautiously, trying to make as little noise as possible in case Psycho is waiting, ready to jump out. So far, I haven't heard or seen anything but my entire body is on alert; every single step sends a panic through my heart.

I'm a fool.

I should have listened to Noah. He must be awake now, and I know he'll be losing his mind. He'll come looking for me, and we could be separated, which is the worst thing that could happen out here. But I realize I can't keep destroying myself for trying to do what's right. There is no right in this situation, everything you do is a choice, and more often than not it's the wrong one.

I can't let my thoughts weaken me. I did the same thing with Nan and I lost Noah. I can't lose him again.

I don't know how long I've been walking, but the sun has shifted, indicating it's the afternoon. If I don't find Noah before sundown, I'll have to spend a night out here alone. Nothing terrifies me more than that. I glance up through the trees at the suspiciously dark clouds hovering, threatening. Even better, I get stuck in a storm with no way out and no protection.

Panic squeezes my heart.

I keep moving.

I reach a fence after another hour and my heart plummets. I've come to a boundary, one of his electrified fences. I don't think there was a boundary near the cave. My entire body starts to tremble as I turn and glance back into the trees I just ventured out of. I can go back in, but I don't even know where the stream is. I'll find it, sure, but how long will that take?

A pained sob leaves my throat and I lower myself to the ground against a tree trunk, trying to steady my breathing. It's no use. I cry so hard everything shakes. My leg hurts, my arm hurts, everything fucking hurts.

I'm tired of pain.

Mostly, I'm tired of fear.

I stay huddled against that tree trunk until I hear a distant bellow. It takes me a few minutes to decipher if it's my imagination or if it's real. It comes again, so distant it's hard to make out. It's a male voice, but is it Noah or is it Bryce? I'm not about to yell back and risk answering the wrong one. I tilt my head to the side and focus. I still can't make it out, so I stand and slowly make my way toward it.

As I move back through the trees, it becomes clearer. It's Noah.

"Noah!" I scream.

"Lara?" he calls, voice deep and frantic.

"I'm here, I'm here!"

I start running down the track toward his voice, happiness and relief flooding my body. I run with little thought, I just need to see him. I need him. I don't think. I'm running, arm clutched against my chest, body focused on one thing—finding him.

Bryce steps out in front of me.

He's grinning, which is the first thing I notice. The second is that he's still got that knife. I stop dead, eyes wide, body seizing with the all-too-familiar panic.

"You two really are the most stupid people I've ever met. Honestly? Screaming out for each other? Did God even give you a brain?"

He has the nerve to use *God* in a sentence? Sick.

"You touch her, I'll kill you."

Noah.

My eyes move over Bryce's shoulder to see him standing, shirtless, powerful, covered in sweat. He's holding his leg slightly off, but otherwise he looks like nothing can bother him. Not a single thing in the world.

Bryce reaches into his jacket, which I now notice is long and hanging down to around his knees. He pulls out a machine gun. My body goes stiff.

"I'm sorry, what?" He laughs, turning so he can see both Noah and me.

"You want a hunt, I'll give you a fucking hunt. But you let her go."

"Noah, no," I yell, terror seizing my chest.

"Giving up his life for hers, honorable," Bryce muses. "I don't honestly know why you'd take such a risk. I mean, it's her fault you're here, after all. If she wasn't enough of a smart-mouth that her grandmother got killed, I'd have never stumbled across her."

Noah snarls.

Bryce laughs, getting his desired reaction. "I must warn you, I'm in somewhat of a foul mood after your little girlfriend here threw rocks at me.

Be careful, Noah. I might accidentally hit something fatal."

No.

"Noah!"

"Run, Lara. Now," he barks.

"No," I scream.

Bryce turns and aims the gun at me. "Do as he says, pet. I'll come for you soon enough."

"No," I cry defiantly.

Bryce spins around and the *pop pop pop* of the machine gun goes off. Bullets fling at my feet and I leap backward with a scream. No pain comes and it takes me a moment to realize it was a warning.

"Run," Noah roars. "Fucking run!"

"Noah." I tremble, scurrying backward as Bryce pulls out his knife and charges toward me.

"I think you need to learn a lesson."

"Lara, run!" Noah yells so loudly, so fiercely that I push to my feet and turn, running.

As I disappear through the forest, the sound of the machine gun rips through my soul.

No.

I left him.

What have I done?

TWENTY-THREE

I'm lost again.

I don't know where I am. It's dark and I'm terrified. I find an overhanging tree and sit beneath it, but it's not protecting me from the vicious storm threatening to roll in. I haven't found the cave. Or the stream. I don't know if Noah is alive. In fact, right now, I know nothing. My entire body is numb; gone is the fear, the pain, the panic. I feel nothing.

In this moment, I think I could die and be okay with it.

Thunder rolls and lightning can be seen slashing across the sky and hitting the ground in the distance. It's coming closer and there is a chance I'm going to get stuck in it. I huddle closer to the tree, praying it'll give me the protection I need, but the truth of the matter is it probably won't.

Imagine that, a storm takes my life after all this fighting?

I laugh bitterly at the thought.

The storm rolls closer and it begins to rain, softly at first and then it comes down hard. It's loud, deafening, and it's freezing cold. I huddle against the tree, but I was right, it isn't enough to protect me from the rain. Branches sway around me, some snapping, and the wind howls through the trees, giving an eerie whistle that makes my skin prickle. I throw my head back and scream. I let it all out. The fear. The pain. The desperation. I scream until my voice goes hoarse and my body gives way.

Then I lie down on my side and curl into a ball, tucking my head into my arms.

After a few minutes, I can't feel the cold from the rain anymore; my body is a numb mess, my mind even worse. Lightning crackles, lighting up the sky. Not enough for me to see anything vital. The shivering starts about ten minutes into the storm and continues until it passes. My skin is soaked, my hair, my body. It feels as though it goes right down to my bones. Maybe it does.

Somehow during that storm, I fall asleep. I don't honestly know how, I think my body has just finally had enough. When I wake, it's to the sound of my name being called. I'm sure it's a dream at first, because there is no possible way Noah is still alive, but after a few minutes I realize that it isn't a dream. He's calling me. I jerk up-right, soaked to the bone and shivering. It's still dark. The rain has stopped, but I can't see a thing.

Is this another trap?

I'll risk it.

"Noah?" I call, my voice hoarse and raspy.

"Lara?"

Oh God, he's alive. Tears, the ones I thought were all dried up, burst forth and run down my cheeks in thick waves.

"Where are you?" he calls.

"I don't, I don't know."

"Keep calling out to me."

For the next ten minutes I call out his name until finally I hear his boots crunching through the leaves. He's coming for me. He's so close.

"I'm here!" I cry happily.

I reach out, I can't see, I can't fucking see, but I reach anyway, hands flying around. Finally, they hit a warm, hard, bare chest. I crumple into his arms. His go around me and we both fall to the ground. My tears run down his skin and my body trembles in his arms.

"You're alive," I sob against him. "You're alive."

"I don't know how, baby. I don't know how."

"H-h-how did you get away?"

"He made a mistake turning to hurt you. I used the rock and hit him over the back of the head just before he turned around once you'd disappeared. Dazed him for a good few minutes. I got a head start. I found a track to the deeper water. I dove in, came out the other side, and went up a tree. By the time he got to me, he couldn't find me."

"How did you find me?"

"A stroke of luck in all this insanity. I was following the track and I thought I saw you over a rise, then I lost you in the darkness so I risked calling out. Fuck, baby, you're soaked."

"I couldn't get out of the storm."

"Me either. I think he's gone back for the night, but we can't be sure. As soon as morning light comes, we're going on the attack guerrilla-style. He might have weapons, but there are two of us and today proved he isn't as smart as he thinks he is. He turned his back on me, the biggest mistake any hunter could make."

I make a strangled sound in my throat. "I honestly thought you were dead."

He makes a raspy sound with his chest and holds me closer. "We've got to take him down, Lara. He's getting desperate."

"I know," I whisper.

"Fuck, baby, being separated from you is something I never want to happen again."

I tremble in his arms.

"Let's try to get some sleep. God only knows when he's going to be back and what he's got planned this time."

I don't even want to think about it.

Little by little, my spirit is dwindling.

I don't know how much longer I can take this.

✦✦✦

They think they've outsmarted me.

They think they actually escaped.

They think I didn't allow it.

I just wanted to give them a moment of hope.

I'm a hunter. I know where my prey is, even if they don't know I'm there.

I know what they're planning.

I'm going to make sure they know I'm in charge. It's time to finish the game.

TWENTY-FOUR

Morning comes.

Forcing my tired body to stand up is one of the hardest things I've had to do. My leg aches, my body aches, my arm is throbbing. Dried blood coats my skin, and my wound desperately needs to be cleaned.

My body is in no shape for a fight, but my mind needs to be. There are no options left.

"Where do we go next?" I ask.

"Higher ground, where we can see him coming. The best spot is back near the waterfall, but instead of hiding inside it, let's wait at the top. If you see any good rocks or spears on the way, grab them. We're going to need them."

We start walking through the forest, eyes peeled for any sign of Bryce. We walk, trenching through the mud created by last night's rain, for hours.

We reach the big dam near the cave and swim over to the rocks leading up into it. We should be able to climb up to the top of the waterfall through the cave. It's the fastest way up. We climb the ledge and with ragged breath push through the waterfall. When we get out the other side, we're so busy rubbing the water from our eyes that we don't notice them. The second our vision clears, an agonized scream is ripped from my throat.

I tumble backward, tripping over a rock.

There are bodies. About five of them. All of them young, teenagers maybe. They've been slaughtered in the most gruesome ways, and there is so much blood. It paints the walls, the bodies, everything. My screams cut off and become agonized little whimpers as I take in the most horrific sight of my life. I can't even make out the gender of some of them, they're that mutilated.

Noah moves. Quickly.

He grabs me, locking his eyes with mine. "You can't fall apart on me, baby. I need you to block it out and keep going." His arm stays around my waist and he hauls me up.

I scale the wall as quickly as I can, which is agonizingly slow. "Take your time, Lara. You've got this," Noah coaxes from behind.

Eventually I haul myself up to the top of the waterfall. I turn and watch Noah come up behind me, but the moment he's over the ledge, his eyes fill with fear.

"Run, we have to ru—"

His voice is cut off when Bryce appears from behind the trees with a shotgun in one hand and a bloodied knife in the other.

"Did you think I wouldn't figure out your next step? I knew all about it. Just like I knew about your little hiding spot. Did you see how I decorated it? Lovely, wasn't it?"

I can't take this. I can't.

Noah pulls me close, but my legs are weak and trembling.

"I must say, it wasn't my usual kill. I just stopped a car and they so gullibly let me in. It was fun, you know. There was this blond girl, she struggled so much as I was slitting her throat." He laughs, shaking his head as if he's telling a story about a child doing something simple, like going to the potty. Not like he just killed innocent young people. "Do you know how much someone bleeds when they're injured? Honestly, it's quite fascinating."

My knees tremble.

"You would have enjoyed it, Lara. You do enjoy watching people die, after all. Tell me, how was your last visit to your nan's grave? Did you apologize? Poor old woman, she had no chance against your smart mouth."

I flinch. Pain rips through my chest.

"Imagine how long and fulfilling her life would have been if you weren't in it to get her killed? You and I, we're no different. I'm just honest about the kind of monster I am."

"Don't listen to him," Noah orders.

"You don't have to listen to me, Lara. You already know it. You're a murderer. Poor Nan."

"Fuck you, asshole," I yell, moving quickly and launching Bryce forward.

We tumble, tumble, tumble. First through the air.

Then we hit the water hard, our bodies sinking beneath the surface. I struggle to come up for air but he's there, too. I know I need to create distance between us now. He probably lost his gun in the fall, but he's too big for me to fight without Noah.

I try to pull away but his arm snakes up and grabs my neck, pushing me under.

I have no breath in my lungs.

Water fills them and I struggle, inhaling way too much.

I reach the surface and sputter, my lungs burning. And again he pushes down. This is it. I'm going to die here. I feel my body growing heavy. Sinking.

Darkness closes in.

"Lara, wake up."

Noah? Is that you?

"Come on. Please wake up."

I'm trying.

"Fuck, don't leave me."

Is he crying?

Oh God. Noah. I can hear you. I'm coming back.

I try to focus on my eyes, but they won't open.

They just won't work. I take a ragged breath, and try again. They flicker.

"Yes, fuck. Baby, please."

I'm almost there.

Another deep breath, and this time I manage to flutter one open. It's blurred, my vision, but I can see the hazy outline of Noah leaning over me. I blink a few more times, getting my other eye open, and I realize I'm on something soft. Really soft, like a bed. I frantically clear my vision and peer around. I don't know where we are. It looks like some sort of room.

"Noah?" I croak.

"Oh thank God," he rasps. "I was worried you wouldn't wake up."

I blink again. "I thought . . . I thought I was going to drown."

He leans down and presses his head against my forehead. "Fuck. I was afraid. You're okay. Are you feeling unwell?"

"Sore, but okay . . . I think. Where are we?"

"I found his hideout," Noah says, voice thick. "It's underground. I noticed an oddly placed shrub and was walking around it, and I realized it was an entrance."

Underground.

Of course it is.

I bolt upright, body screaming in pain. "Where is he? Is he dead?"

Noah shakes his head. "I don't think so. I bashed his head with a rock once I reached you in the water, but you went under and he got away while I was bringing you to shore. Didn't get his bike, though. I saw it at the waterfall and drove us a safe distance away, then happened upon this place. I hid the bike in the bushes, I don't want him to know we're here."

I study the space. It's big, considering its location. It has rustic wooden walls, no windows, and a staircase going upward to what looks like an exit. There is a bed, a sofa, a small kitchenette, and a bath. There are also televisions everywhere, lining one entire wall. The other wall has a closet that's open, and I can see that it's full of military-style clothing and tactical gear. A desk in the corner is stacked with papers, clippings about my nan and Noah's time with the fire station, and pictures of the two of us arguing, together, running, all of it.

"This space is making me feel ill," I rasp.

"I know, but it's the only place we can be right now where we can anticipate him. He's injured. It can finally be over."

"Are there any weapons?"

He gets a troubled look on his face. "Yes, one knife." He pulls it from his waistband and hands it to me. I clutch it likes it's the Holy Grail. "Bryce isn't a man to make stupid decisions, so either his leaving this here was a mistake . . . or he planted it here, knowing we would come."

"Do you have a feeling one way or the other?"

He shakes his head. "Impossible to tell."

I look down at my leg and see that my shin is

covered in clean white gauze. "You found bandages?"

"First aid, yeah. Peroxide and antibacterial ointment, too. I cleaned us both up. I also found food and water. You need to drink and eat a little."

"Phone?" I ask hopefully.

"No communication out. He's not stupid."

"What do we do now? Just wait for him to show up?"

"If he knows we're here. If not, this is the perfect place to ambush him. That's why I turned off all the lights and hid the bike. This is our last chance to end this."

"And when we do, how do we get out?"

"I disabled the electric fences. When he's dead, we'll find a way out past them."

"I feel like we're closer than ever to being free."

"Thanks to you, brave girl." He squeezes my hand. "Your nan would be proud."

I smile at the thought of her.

"Remember the first time you met her?" I say, trying to change the subject.

He smiles and nods.

"Nan, this is Noah," I say.

Nan has just stepped into my house, a container of cookies in her hands, when she stops dead and looks up at Noah.

"This is the man you were telling me about?" she asks, squinting.

I inwardly giggle. She likes to act tough but my old nan is the sweetest woman in the world.

"Yes. Noah, this is my nan."

Noah steps forward and extends his hand. "Lovely to meet you. Lara has told me so much about you."

Nan sets the cookies down and takes his hand. "Do you have a criminal record, Noah?"

He blinks. "Ah. No."

"Ever stolen something?"

"No ma'am."

"Ever hurt an animal or a child?"

I press a hand to my mouth to stop my giggle.

"Of course not," Noah says, his lips twitching.

"You going to hurt my granddaughter?"

"Not if I can help it."

She narrows her eyes, but her lips twitch. "Which baseball team do you root for? Be careful how you answer, Noah. I'm picky."

"The Cubs, ma'am."

She smiles. Nan loves the Cubs. She might not live anywhere near them, but she's a diehard fan.

"Pizza or pasta?"

I'm giggling hysterically now.

"Pizza."

Nan lets him go with a huge smile on her face and turns to me. "I like him, you can keep him."

Noah is laughing when I snap out of the memory. "She was the coolest lady I've ever met."

I laugh. "She was. I'm glad you got to meet her."

"Me too, Lara. Me too. Now get some sleep," he says. "We need our strength for what's coming."

He turns out the lights and lies back down beside me.

I close my eyes and think of my nanna, smiling as another memory comes back to me. She always wanted me to believe in myself. She embraced my confident side.

"There's nothing wrong with being confident, Lara, but don't be cocky. Nobody likes a cocky person."

"The world is such an ugly place, Nan," I say, *crossing my legs on her sofa. "I think sometimes you do have to be cocky; otherwise you get pushed around."*

"You make a good point, dear, but there is also something else you can be."

I raise my brows. "Don't leave me hanging, Nanna."

She smiles. So beautiful. "You can be kind. You can be brave. You can be loyal. You can be strong. No matter how ugly the world is, if you're that beautiful it can't get past you."

I smile. "I don't know if I'm any of those things, but I'd love to be."

She comes and sits beside me. "You're all of those things and more, Lara. You're the kindest girl I know. Look how often you come over here and look after me. You're the bravest girl I know. I admit you're a little too loud sometimes, but you go into the world fighting and that makes you something else. You are more than loyal, we both know that. Mostly you're strong. The strongest girl I know. You could endure anything, anything at all. I believe it with all that I am. Be all those things, Lara, and the world will give you what you need."

Tears run down my cheeks. I dip my head.

Nanna believed in me. She believed in me.

And I know now, I know more than anything, that if she were here she'd tell me that I have to find all those things—I have to find who I am—and I have to embrace them. She'd tell me I'm not weak, that I'm not a bad person, that it wasn't my fault. God, she'd probably slap me if she knew how much I let her death eat me up, change me, take away who I was.

I have to forgive myself.

I know it now more than ever.

Old Lara is back, and I have to hang on to her with both hands.

But first, Noah and I are going to get out of here.

Bryce is going to come. I know it, I feel it.

I'm getting us out of here.

TWENTY-FIVE
—Bryce—

What kind of stupid people go into a place where I can trap and kill them?

I chuckle to myself as I stand outside the door to my hideout. I can hear them talking. Honestly, whose bright idea was this? They just threw themselves in my path and made it easy for me to kill them. She's practically dead already, he's exhausted; they swore they wouldn't end up falling into my game, but they did. I didn't count on them working together like they did, but it's no matter. It'll only hurt worse when they watch each other die.

Idiots.

They were never going to beat me.

I reach into my pocket and pull out a lighter. Time to draw them out and end this once and for all. I move around to the back of my hideout, lifting another small door that opens up a compartment where I keep some weapons. I pull out a massive hunting knife, much bigger than the one I left for them. I could just shoot them, but I want to see them squirm, fight, plead. Yes, a gun is no fun. I tuck another two knives into my belt, just in case. Then I pull out a bottle of gas.

I walk over to the back of my hideout and pour it on, then I light it up.

Grinning, I walk around to the front door and stand, waiting.

I'll take Noah down first, or maybe I'll take Lara down and watch him suffer. So many choices. Anticipation bubbles in my chest as I wait. In a matter of minutes, the front door swings up and they come scrambling out, him holding her by the arm as he pulls her. Always the hero.

"I wondered which one of you had the bright idea of hiding in the place I know best. I'm guessing you, Noah."

Noah stops dead and turns toward me, his face wild with anger. He drops his hold on Lara's arm. He looks scared. Finally he looks fucking scared. So he should—he's about to die. Slowly. His hand moves quickly, and I see the exact moment that he realizes he doesn't have a weapon. Maybe he dropped it. I'm guessing he dropped it. I laugh hysterically. "What happened, Noah? Did you drop your weapon?"

"I don't need a weapon to beat you," Noah growls. "I'm a fucking man, not a coward like you."

I laugh. "Funny that. Yes, you're such a man you couldn't even get your precious little girlfriend out of here."

My eyes flick to Lara again. She looks defeated. Good.

"Looks like your little woman is giving up, Noah. I wondered how long it would take for her to break."

Noah looks to Lara and his eyes flash. "Lara?"

"I'm sorry, Noah," Lara whispers. "I tried. I'm just so tired. So sick of fighting. It's over. I can't . . ."

"Lara!" Noah tries to take a step forward but I get in his way.

"Get out of my fucking way," he barks. "I'll kill you."

I laugh, throwing my head back. Then I aim my knife and with precision, I throw it. Noah tries to move out of the way but it ends up wedged in his leg. He drops to the ground. Lara screams. I focus on Noah, walking slowly toward him. He's hissing in pain as he jerks the knife out. I reach around to my pants and pull out another knife.

"I'll fucking kill you," Noah hisses, pressing a hand to the blood and clutching the knife with the other.

"Now it's a fair match," I say, and my eyes catch sight of Lara.

She is clutching her wrist and there is blood trickling out from her fingers. A bloodied knife falls on the floor beside her. She starts swaying.

Weak. Little. Bitch.

"Would you look at that, Noah?" I laugh. "Your little woman is trying to take the easy way out."

Noah's head whips around and I watch the exact moment all the color drains from his face as he realizes what she's doing. Lara is trying to kill herself so I don't have to do it for her. Smart. But weak. So pathetic. The useless waste of space. I always knew she didn't have it in her. She sways again. She's making this too fucking easy. I should go over there and drive this knife into her heart. I can't believe she thinks she can take this away from me.

But Noah's pain is too good.

It's too real.

Excitement floods my body as I watch him breaking right in front of me. The pain in his face has my body coming alive. This isn't how I wanted everything to go, but I'm always up for a slight direction change. This will make Noah angry, but weak. He'll want to fight me. He'll want to hurt me. But he will lose.

"Lara?" Noah says, his voice betrayed and hurt. "Lara!"

"Oh for God's sake," I bark at her. "You're not seriously going to pass out, are you? At least try to give me the fight I've been waiting for."

"Noah," she croaks. "I'm so sorry . . ."

She drops to her knees.

"Lara," Noah yells, his voice frantic. Aw. He doesn't want to lose her.

How very tragic.

Her eyes roll and she falls backward. I study her chest. Her breathing is so shallow it's about to stop. She must have slit that vein good. I guess she's tougher than I thought if she had it in her to do that. Still. Fucking bitch ruined my endgame.

"Seriously?" I bellow, throwing a hand up. "I fucking create this game only for that bitch to fucking die by her own hand."

"Lara," Noah screams, getting up and running over to her and dropping to his knees. "Lara!"

"I mean honestly," I bark, stalking toward Noah. "I fucking knew she was weak, but to kill herself and leave you behind? I thought she loved you a little more than that."

"Lara, wake up," Noah bellows, tears running down his pathetic cheeks.

"Waste of my fucking time," I mutter to myself as I reach Noah. "Stupid weak bitch. Get up. I'm going to make my game worthwhile, even if it fucking kills me."

Noah leaps up and with a feral roar throws himself at me.

Finally, someone with some spirit.

Time to die, Noah.

TWENTY-SIX
—Noah—

She killed herself.

I can't believe she's fucking gone.

Tears run down my cheeks as I shake her life-less body. I should have known she was struggling. I was so fucking busy ignoring her that I didn't realize she was quiet, too quiet. I want to press my cheek to her chest, I want to hear her fucking heartbeat, but I don't get a chance. I just want one fucking more second.

Lara, no.

I can't live a life without her. Flashes of her smiling and laughing fill my mind, and my heart threatens to explode. I'll never see any of that again. I let out a ragged cry and it feels like someone has a fist around my heart, squeezing, suffocating the life out of me. How dare you give up on me, Lara? Fuck, how dare you fucking leave me? A strangled sob gets trapped in my throat as pain unlike anything I've ever felt in my life tears through my body. Losing her once was hard enough. But losing her again . . . like this. I'll never be okay without her. My beautiful lady.

Lara. Baby. Come back.

"Waste of my fucking time," Bryce mutters to himself as he approaches behind me. "Stupid weak bitch. Get up. I'm going to make my game worthwhile, even if it fucking kills me."

I see red. Anger flashes in my eyes, my ears ring, and I know, I just know I'm going to kill him. Slowly. Painfully. I'm going to rip his fucking heart out with my bare hands. I leap up and spin around with a feral roar, throwing myself at him. I slam against his body with a loud thump and we both topple backward. He might not be as big as me, but he's strong; more than that, he's a good fighter.

"Why so angry at me, Noah?" he taunts, driving his knee upward and sending me stumbling back with a roar. "She's the one who took her own life."

"Shut the fuck up," I bellow, rolling and then throwing myself back at him.

"You knew it all along, didn't you? You knew she was weak. You knew she was pathetic. You knew she could never do it. So did I. I always knew she'd let you down, that she'd fail you. God, she's so fucking weak, isn't she? It's laughable."

I drive a fist into his face, and with a wild laugh

his head jerks backward. He reaches into his jacket and pulls out another knife, a massive one. I don't fucking care. I don't even know where the one I had has gone. I don't care if he kills me, so long as I make him fucking suffer first. I can do that with my bare hands.

"I'll fucking make you pay," I snarl, punching him again.

He swings the knife, narrowly missing me. I roll off but he's quick and throws himself onto me before I can even get to my feet, slamming my face into the dirt. Agony tears through me as my nose crunches and blood fills my mouth. I throw my head backward, slamming it into his jaw. He goes off with a growl, and I launch to my feet, blood running down my face.

My eyes flick to Lara, who is lifeless on the ground, and I roar with agony and pain, but mostly with heartbreak.

"Yeah," he taunts, waving the knife around, blood dripping from his mouth. "Look at her. Look at how she let you down. Look at how she failed you."

I lunge at him again, and he slashes the knife. It glides across my stomach, opening my skin. Pain overtakes my body and my vision blurs for a moment. I blink rapidly, trying to gather myself as warm blood trickles down me. He slams into me again and then I'm falling. I hit the ground, back smacking against the dirt. He stands over me as I try to gather myself, laughing, fucking laughing.

"I thought you had more go in you, Noah. Honestly I did. But I always knew that little bitch would fail and that would be the thing to break you." He runs his finger over the blade as I try to get up. He puts a boot to my chest, pushing me back down so hard my head bounces off the ground. "You two thought you had it over me, didn't you? Hilarious, really. I knew exactly what I was picking when I found you both. And here you were thinking your love would save you."

He throws his head back and laughs.

I lie there panting.

I fucking hate him.

"How pathetic," he says in a singsong voice, using the back of his hand to wipe his nose. "She didn't love you. Stupid bitch didn't love anything but herself. She only cared about"—he raises a hand and makes air quotes—"her 'problems.' She killed her own grandmother with her smart mouth, and yet you believed in her. Didn't you?"

He laughs again.

My heart fucking twists. It feels like it's being ripped out of my chest.

I shoot my hand out quickly, hoping to catch him off guard, but he moves like lightning, stabbing the knife into my hand and pinning it into the dirt. I bellow in agony, blinding pain ripping through my body.

"I'm going to kill you," he says, straddling me and leaning down close. "I'm going to rip your fucking heart out. I'm going to stuff it in your mouth so when they find you, they'll know that you fucked up, that you gave it to the wrong woman and that's what got you killed. You're pathetic, Noah. But she's worse."

He raises the knife over my chest and I stare at it, just stare. I want him to kill me. I want him to fucking kill me. I don't care anymore. He can take it all. I've got nothing left. She left me with fucking nothing. She gave up on me. Goddammit, fuck you, Lara. I believed in you. I believed you were strong enough and you let me down.

"Bye bye, Noah."

I close my eyes.

Finally, it's over.

TWENTY-SEVEN
—Lara—

From the second we stepped out of the hideout, I knew what I was going to do. I thought about it while Noah slept. I knew Bryce would fall for it because he believes I'm weak, he believes it with everything he is. I was right. All I had to do was make a cut on my wrist, away from the vein, that bled enough for them to believe I'd taken my own life. Falling to the ground was easy. Shallowing my breathing wasn't hard.

They ate it up.

I hate knowing Noah is taking this so hard. Hearing his pain killed me, but if I told him my plan he would have never gone for it. I don't know how much more we could fight Bryce, as injured as we are. When he hit Noah's leg with the knife, and I saw the pain on Noah's face, I knew my plan was the right one. Noah will understand, but right now, right now . . . I have to end this. For both of us.

I grip the knife that I let fall beside me and stand, watching Bryce hovering over Noah, who is looking up at him like he's given up. He's given up because of me. Because I let him down. He thinks I'm dead. He thinks that I gave up. But I didn't. I knew exactly what I was doing. Bryce thinks he has me pegged—hell, maybe he does. He thinks that I'm the reason this failed, but he's wrong. I'm going to be the reason we win.

Bryce raises the knife and Noah closes his eyes. I lunge.

I do it without thought. I raise the knife and drive it into Bryce's back, knocking him flat over Noah, who starts struggling immediately.

"Wha—" Bryce gasps.

I lean down as I twist the knife in his back. "Never, ever turn your back on your victim unless you're sure she's dead. I thought you were smart enough to at least check."

I pull the knife out and drive it back in. He slumps farther down, croaking in agony.

"You never, ever fucking underestimate someone."

I pull it out and drive it in again, ignoring the crushing of bones and squelching of blood.

"And you never, fucking ever, touch what's mine."

I pull the knife back out and let Bryce roll off Noah. I stand, using my foot to kick him to his back. Noah rolls to his hands and knees, staring at me, shock registering on his face. I have to end this for him. For us. No longer will I hurt another person in my life because I don't know who I am. Right here, right now, I know exactly who I am. I'm Lara, strong and a little soft—a perfect mixture of both.

I straddle Bryce, who is spluttering, blood pouring from his mouth. He looks up at me with shock, but mostly awe. Clearly he didn't think I had it in me. Neither did Noah. Neither did I. But I did. I've had it in me all along.

"You didn't think I had it in me, did you?" I say, staring into his pathetic eyes. "You thought I'd let him down. You thought I'd fail. You were so sure."

I raise the knife and his eyes flare.

"But the thing about me, Bryce, is some way, somehow, I always fucking bounce back. You helped me realize that. Your game was meant to weaken me, but you know what it did? It made me strong."

I slam the knife down into his heart and watch as his body jerks beneath me and his last breath wheezes from his lungs.

"I win," I whisper.

Then my world goes black.

TWENTY-EIGHT

When I wake, I'm in Noah's arms and he's carrying me. It takes my mind a few minutes to realize where I am. When I remember what I did, I gasp and begin to squirm. "Hush," Noah says, his voice exhausted. "It's over."

"Noah," I croak.

"Over, baby."

"I k-k-killed him."

He stops and sets me down. I don't know where we are. I don't know anything except that Bryce is dead, and I killed him.

Noah cups my face. We're both covered in blood, most of it our own, some of it his. Noah's face is messed up, dried blood all over his skin. "You saved me. You fucking saved me. Us. I don't have a single word that can express how fucking incredible you were back there."

"I killed . . ." My voice shakes as reality sets in.

Noah slams his lips against mine. "We're breathing because of you, you beautiful, brave, perfect woman."

We are.

We're breathing because of me.

Tears run down my cheeks. "We're free."

He clutches my hand. "We're free. Now we need to find a way out of here or we're going to bleed to death. You didn't save our lives for us to die out here."

Save our lives.

I saved our lives.

"I'm sorry I let you believe I was dead."

Noah stops and turns to me. "You're a genius, Lara. You found a strength even I couldn't have mustered. To do what you did, so perfectly—I have no fucking words except thank you." His voice breaks. "Because I don't think we would have gotten out of there without you."

I swallow and nod, shock slowly starting to creep into my body.

"We need to get out of here," he says, tugging my hand.

I put one foot in front of the other, and I walk. I walk until we find a quiet road. By the time we stumble out onto it, I'm numb. From head to toe, I can't feel anything. I feel as though I'm existing without actually being aware. Shock. Reality. Horror. All of it has finally set in. I guess that's what happens when you've spent so long living in fear. When it's gone, you just have nothing left.

Noah is clutching my hand like he has been for the past two hours, but neither of us has spoken a single word. The horror of the last week is replaying in our minds, over and over, tormenting us, torturing us, reminding us that while we escaped the monster . . . will we ever escape the nightmare? Will killing him torture me? Right now I feel nothing, but will it always be that way?

Car lights flash in our direction, snapping us out of our daze, and we turn to face them. For a moment, I don't think whoever is driving is willing to stop for us. I can only imagine how we look. Half naked, injured, bloodied, and feral. The vehicle slows, though, and eventually pulls off to the side of the road. My knees start wobbling and for a second I'm not sure I can even take the few steps toward the car.

An older man gets out, his wife shuffling out the other side. I worry they'll get a closer look at us and run, but they don't. The older man squints, and then his mouth drops open. "It's . . . Maggie, it's them."

Them.

We have a title?

"Oh my good Lord," Maggie gasps, rushing over and putting her hands on my shoulders without hesitation. She doesn't care that I'm bloodied or half naked. "It's them. They're alive. Peter, get the blanket from the trunk. Hurry. They're freezing."

"Y-y-y-you know who we are?" I croak.

Is that my voice? It doesn't sound like my voice.

"Of course, dear. Your face has been all over the news for a week."

It has?

Then why didn't anyone find us?

I chastise myself for such an awful thought. I don't even know where we are. I don't know how far away from Orlando we are. How was anyone supposed to know where we were? I squeeze Noah's hand, but he doesn't squeeze back. Is he too far gone? Am I too far gone? Will we ever recover from this?

"Lara, right?" Maggie asks as Peter gets the blanket from the trunk.

"Yes," I croak.

She looks to Noah. "And Noah."

He nods. No words.

"I'm not going to ask what happened to you both, because it's none of my business, I'm just going to get you to a hospital. Come, climb into the car and I'll pass the blanket in. You must be freezing."

I wouldn't know if I'm cold anymore; truthfully, it's hard to tell what I feel. My body has gone beyond pain, beyond feeling. It's just dead. Numb. Broken.

Noah jerks me toward the car and we slide in. The warmth from the heater tickles my face, and I close my eyes. I didn't realize just how cold I was until this very second. Noah climbs in beside me and Maggie leans in, handing us a blanket. I take it, running my fingers over the soft edges. I would have never noticed how it felt against my skin before; now it's all I can think about.

I bring it up to my chin, and I start shivering, even though I'm warm.

Noah does the same.

Maggie and Peter get into the car, and she orders him to drive to the nearest hospital.

"H-h-h-how far away from Orlando are we?" I ask, my voice hoarse.

"Just over an hour, dear."

An hour? One measly hour?

I close my eyes. Noah has let go of my hand and I want it back, I want him to hang on to me and never let me go, but he's shutting down and I don't blame him. We've lived through hell, and the entire time we were in it, we were fighting to get out. Now that we're out, nothing feels okay. There seems to be little relief, little comfort, little of anything.

We're free, alive, and safe.

But it doesn't feel okay.

Maggie asks us basic questions as we drive, but only I answer. Noah stays silent. Eventually the entire car falls silent and we all just sit there. I can smell us, and I only realized now that we have a strong scent coming from our bodies. Blood, sweat, days without hygiene, and death. So much death. I close my eyes and take a shaky breath. I'm not ready for this. I have to be, but I'm not.

The questions.

The panicked family members.

The normal life.

The car slows and I realize we're already at the hospital. I didn't notice any lights; I didn't even hear the cars around us. Somehow, I blanked out all of it. I was so far gone in my own little world I didn't even realize we'd come back to civilization. Panic grips me as I peer out the window to where Maggie is calling for a nurse, waving her arms around. One comes out and listens as she rambles quickly.

About us, obviously.

The nurse nods and rushes back inside, coming out with two wheelchairs. Here goes the silence; in seconds it's going to rush out the door and we're going to be bombarded with questions and concerns and needles and doctors. I take another shaky breath and look to Noah. He's staring straight ahead. My heart aches for him. I don't get to say anything because the door is flung open and a young, blond nurse peeks inside the car.

She takes one look at us and her eyes go wide. "Oh my."

That about sums it up.

"My name is Jill. I'm going to help you out of the car, okay? Can you tell me if anything is broken?"

I shake my head.

"And him?"

I shake my head again.

"Okay, very carefully hop out for me. Lara, is it?"

Does she watch the news, too?

I climb out of the car, ignoring her question. She takes hold of my arm, directing me into a wheelchair. It's cold against my legs, but another nurse quickly rushes forward and hands me a warm blanket. I raise it back up to my chin and keep it there, watching as Noah climbs out. He gets the same treatment. Then we're being wheeled inside.

I look over my shoulder and smile at Maggie.

She sobs.

I don't know why.

TWENTY-NINE

I wake to the sounds of frantic voices.

Nurses are calling out to one another, and the sound of male cries can be heard echoing through the halls. Familiar male cries. I sit up, rubbing my eyes and pushing myself from the bed. Noah and I have been in here overnight but I've yet to see him. When we arrived we were whisked away for assessing and questioning. I've been worried about him ever since. My feet hit the cold ground, and for a few seconds I wobble about. The nurse took my drip out today; I'm now hydrated, so I don't have to drag that horrible thing around with me anymore.

"Please, sir, calm down!" I hear a nurse cry.

"Get the fuck away from me."

Noah.

That's Noah.

My heart pounds and I rush to the door.

"If you don't calm down we'll have to detain you."

"Get off me!"

I pick up the pace, running down the hall on weak legs toward the pained, broken voice of my love. I reach the room where nurses are rushing in and out, and I step in.

"Lara, you can't be here, it's dangerous," a young nurse says, taking my arm.

I glare at her. "You know nothing about what he's going through. Let me in there."

"I can't do that—" she begins, but I jerk my arm back so hard she stumbles.

I take the window of opportunity and run into the room. Two male doctors or nurses, I don't know which, are holding Noah's arms. One is coming over to jab a needle in his neck.

"Stop!" I cry, running over.

"Miss, you need to leave," the doctor yells.

"No. Stop. He's just afraid. You're making it worse."

Noah throws his head back and bellows, sweat trickling down his face. He needs me. I wasn't there for him when he needed me last, but I am now and I won't give up on him.

"Let him go," I say to the two men holding him.

"Can someone get her out," one yells.

I ignore them, climbing onto the end of Noah's bed. His legs are jerking, but my weight holds them down.

"Miss, get off the bed!"

I crawl up and when I reach his face, I cup it in my hands. "Noah, stop."

He keeps thrashing.

"Get someone in here to move her!" the doctor orders. "Now!"

"Noah, please," I say.

He keeps bellowing.

I lean in closer, risking a solid head butt. I bring my mouth to his ear, my legs straddling his hips. "Noah. Calm down," I say softly into his ear. "It's me. Lara. I'm here. You're okay. I'm here with you. You're safe now."

His body jerks, but he stops thrashing.

"It's all over," I continue. "It's okay. It's finished. We're safe. I'm here. I won't leave you. I promise you I'll never leave you again."

His sweat runs down his face, but he's stopped thrashing. The two men slowly let him go, and the doctor waves a hand to make sure they don't go far. Noah jerks in my grip. Then his big arms close around me, consuming me, keeping me safe. I sob, burrowing my face into the crook of his neck. He starts shaking. Finally breaking. He's been a pillar of strength, so strong, so determined, and now it's all finally crumbling.

"Leave them be," the doctor orders. "Nurse, stay by the door."

The room clears. Noah hangs on to me so tightly I can hardly breathe, but I say nothing. We just sit there, both of us crying, me loudly, him silently.

After about an hour, his arms finally relax and he says in a thick, emotional tone, "I can't close my eyes and not see you lying there bleeding."

My heart breaks.

"I know," I whisper.

"The dreams are so real. I think I'm back there, that we're still trapped and fighting. In them, he always kills you right in front of me. It's so fucking real, Lara."

"I know, honey."

"Then I wake up and I realize it's over, but I don't feel any better."

"I think it's going to take some time for us to feel better."

"I don't know what happened just now, it was like I couldn't rise from the dream. They just wanted to hold me down and the more they did, the more frantic I got. Then I heard your voice . . ."

I lean back and meet his bloodshot eyes. He looks awful. Worn out. I probably look the same. "I'm here, Noah. I let you down in that forest. I let a moment of weakness beat me, but you can be assured it'll never happen again. I'm never going to leave you. Never. We're going to get through this together."

"They want us to go back," he croaks.

"I know."

"I can't . . ."

I nod. "I know."

"It's all over the news."

I sigh and press my cheek to his chest. "Yeah, Rachel told me. Apparently a nurse from here talked."

"Of course."

"What are we going to do, Noah? How is this ever going to feel okay again?"

He wraps his big arms around me and falls silent a moment. "I don't know."

"Me either."

"All I know is the time without you was hell. I need you here with me, Lara. I can't do this without you."

"If that's where you need me, that's where I'll be."

"And when we leave?" he asks. I stiffen in his arms.

I hadn't thought of that. We're not going to be in this hospital forever. We both have apartments and jobs—and the very idea of going back to those alone terrifies me. What the hell are we going to do? A week ago we were nothing, now we're something, but how much of a something are we? Are we going somewhere with this or are we taking it slow . . .

I decide to go with honesty and see where that ends up for me. "I don't know how I can go home alone."

He exhales shakily. "Neither do I."

"So what do we do?"

"I want you to come home with me. My apartment is close to yours, we can go back and forth when we need to, but I want you with me, Lara. I can't stand the thought of being without you again."

"Then that's what we'll do."

"I've got you in this, please know that. Nobody will ever touch you again."

"I know that," I whisper.

"Stay with me?"

"Always, Noah."

He had my back when my nan died; now it's my turn to have his. And I will, for as long as we're both breathing, I'll do everything I can to protect him as staunchly as he protected me.

Always.

THIRTY

"Can you tell us what it was like out there?"
"How did you get out?"
"How did you survive?"
"Did you kill him?"
"What did he do to you?"

Reporters, flashes from cameras, people everywhere. I'm stiff, feet planted firmly on the ground, refusing to move forward. Noah tugs my arm, using the other hand to push through the crowds of reporters waiting for us outside the hospital as we leave. It's been a week. In that time, we've had our wounds treated, we've been interviewed by the police countless times, and Noah and I were able to visit each other in our rooms. We both decided to stay together at his apartment once we got out. Neither of us could stand the thought of being without each other again.

Now we hold hands and face the hordes of reporters clamoring for details. They've no doubt been waiting for us to come out so they can get the answers to their questions.

"No comment," Noah growls, shoving through them until we reach the car waiting for us.

My dad gets out, opening the door and helping me into the vehicle. Noah jumps in the front and then we're off. My heart is pounding and I drop my head into my hands and try to steady out my breathing.

"That's going to happen for a while," Dad says. "Are you two okay with all the fuss?"

"Yeah," Noah mutters. "Lara, are you okay?"

I don't lift my head from my hands.

"Lara, honey?"

I look up, tears running down my cheeks. Noah doesn't hesitate: He unbuckles and climbs into the back. His arms go around me and he pulls me tight as I sob. I hate it. I hate all of this.

"It won't be like this forever."

"They're vultures," I sob. "They don't care about what we went through at all."

"No, they don't. They just want a story."

"We'll keep you safe," Dad says from the front. "I promise."

I nestle into Noah's chest the entire ride to his apartment. It's quiet when we arrive, thank God. We climb out of the car and Mom and Rachel come rushing out, smiling and opening their arms for us. I rush forward and throw myself in, relishing in the comfort they're bringing.

"The apartment is cleaned, stocked, and ready to go. You don't need to leave for weeks if you don't want to." Rachel smiles, stepping back. She's been a godsend this past week. Visiting me at the hospital every day and bringing me anything I needed.

"I've even put four apple pies in the freezer," Mom adds with a smile.

"Thank you both so much," I whisper, running a hand through my hair and looking up at the two-story apartment.

"It's very much appreciated," Noah says. "But would you mind if we did this part alone?"

"Of course!" Mom says, hugging him tight. "Of course."

"Call us if you need anything," Rachel says, hugging me again. She smiles at Noah and he nods to her.

Then they're gone.

We stand at the front door, silently.

"Are you ready?"

"As I'll ever be," I whisper.

Noah reaches out and takes my hand. We step inside.

The apartment smells of freshly cooked pies and feels far homier than I would have thought. I look around. Since Noah and I both left our old apartment after we split, I haven't seen his new place, but it's nice. Modern, spacious, and filled with very masculine furniture. I walk into the large black-and-white-decorated kitchen and open the fridge. It's full to the brim with premade meals and food.

I smile.

Bless them.

"Are you tired?" Noah asks, coming up behind me and wrapping his arms around my waist.

"Yeah," I say softly. "So damned tired."

"It's been hard sleeping, huh?" he says, nuzzling my neck softly.

"I know it's over, I'm so glad, but it's still really hard to close my eyes and not wait for that sound."

"It'll go away, eventually. At least we're out of that damned hospital."

"I think that's the worst part about escape, you know?"

He looks down at me, pressing a kiss to my forehead. "What's that?"

"When you escape, you kind of just want time alone to recover. But people, they want answers. They're everywhere. Doctors. Police. Then there are the hospitals."

"I hear what you're saying," he murmurs. "But we're here now, and not there."

"And we have each other," I point out softly, reaching up and stroking his jaw.

"So what do you say we go get some sleep, *together?*"

My heart flutters. "I would love that."

He takes my hand and leads me into his bedroom. I stare at the familiar bed and my heart warms. We both strip down, removing our clothes. Then we climb into the bed and curl into each other. This is the only way we feel okay at the moment; for some reason, it brings us comfort. Probably because the only time we felt safe in that horrible place was when we were in each other's arms.

"I love you, Lara," Noah whispers against the back of my neck.

"I love you, too."

And for the first time in weeks, I fall asleep thinking maybe, just maybe, things might be okay.

Maybe.

THIRTY-ONE

I shove the spear out in front of me. "Don't come near me," I yell, my voice betraying me by coming out weak and shaky.

He laughs again, flashing white teeth in my direction. "Really, Lara."

I take a step back. He grins and moves closer. "I think I should remove something from your body, something essential. Say, a finger? What do you think?"

I say nothing. I just lunge. It's stupid. I don't realize it at the time but the second I crash against him, I know I've made a mistake. He's bigger than he looks, and his body is solid muscle. I'm tiny and weak; I have no idea how to use a spear. The wooden object just tumbles out of my hand when it makes contact with his body, and I'm left with nothing.

Laughter fills my ears as he takes hold of my hand, jerking me closer.

"No," I scream. "No!"

With a wild, feral laugh, he brings the knife closer. I squirm, thrash, and kick, but he's strong and he's not letting go. I scream and pull as hard as I can, but it's no use.

"Lara! Hey!"

I jerk upright, sweat running down my face and soaking the blankets. It's dark. Where am I? Panic grips my chest and I start feeling around frantically, trying to figure out what's going on. Is he here? Oh God. Did he find me? I thought I was safe? How did he find me so quickly? Noah? Noah!

"Lara!"

My teeth chatter as my body is shaken. I blink a few times, slowly coming to. A soft bed beneath me. Noah's hands on my shoulders. It's over. Bryce is dead. We're okay. We're safe. We got out. I killed him. *I killed him.*

"Noah?" I croak. "Is he . . . is he gone?"

"Baby, he's gone. You're okay. It was a dream."

A dream.

Just a dream.

"It was so real," I croak. "I was taking sleeping pills in the hospital and I didn't dream, Noah, I didn't dream. I want it to go away. I don't want to see that every time I close my eyes."

"It'll get easier to handle," he says, running his fingers down my hair. "It will, baby. I swear."

"Will I hear him for the rest of my life? See him around every corner? Every time I close my eyes?"

"No," he says, softly. "No you won't."

I nuzzle into him, needing him, needing the closeness. I don't ever want to be without him. I need him to make it go away. To make me feel better. To make it feel like it never happened. To take my mind away for just a second.

"Noah," I whisper, trembling in his arms. "Make love to me."

"Lara," he groans. "I don't . . ."

"Please. I need you. I need that. The only pure, beautiful thing he couldn't take from us. We're going to have to relive this again tomorrow at the police station. So please. Give me this."

He turns his head. I tilt mine back and his lips graze over mine, softly at first but slowly increasing in pressure until our mouths crush together in a slow, deep frenzy. He moves, tucking me beneath his big body, and our mouths don't part as he shifts between my legs. His skin is pressed against mine, so hot, so hard, and he feels so good. He's right there, pressing against my entrance. Hard and ready.

His mouth pulls away from mine and trails down my jaw and neck, stopping at my collarbone before dipping to my breasts. He sucks softly on one nipple, then the other, drawing each into his mouth. His hands caress, gently, passionately, and all the while his erection rubs up and down my sex, taunting me, teasing me. I whimper into his mouth when his lips find mine again and his hand tangles in my hair, tilting my head back so he can trail kisses down my throat.

"Please," I whimper. "Please, Noah."

"Please what?" he growls, nipping my jaw.

"I need you inside me."

"Then that's what you'll get."

He reaches down, hooking my leg around his hips, and then he's sliding inside me, inch by agonizing inch. So big, so hard. I gasp and my fingers run down his back, lightly caressing his skin as he fills me. He feels incredible, so big and strong. So powerful and dominant. His hand is still tangled in my hair and his fingers move along my scalp as he clenches and unclenches with pleasure.

"Noah," I gasp, arching up to meet him.

"Fuck. Yes," he grunts, filling me completely.

Then he makes love to me, slow and steady at first, hands, mouths, bodies colliding. Then frenzy takes over and my nails glide down his skin, his hand tugs on my hair, and our lovemaking becomes fucking. Furious, intense fucking. I arch up to him, screaming his name as an orgasm unlike any other rocks my body, taking me over. My legs quiver, my knees wobble, my palms get sweaty, and I cry out his name as bliss consumes me.

His orgasm follows close behind, matching my own in intensity: His body arches, his muscles clench, and he grunts out a name before dropping his forehead to mine. We feel no pain. Not a single thing on our bodies hurts in this moment, even though they should. We've had so much pain, nothing can compare. Nothing. He's all I need, he's all I see, he's all I feel, and I'll be okay with having that forever.

"If that's what we need to do to make the nightmares go away," he murmurs against my lips, "I vote we do it all the time."

I laugh softly. "Me too."

Me too.

THIRTY-TWO

"I'm nervous," I whisper, climbing out of the car and staring around at the road we have to cross to get to the police station.

"It'll be okay. One day we have to learn how to get on with our lives, Lara. Today is that day," Noah says, helping me to my feet and clutching my hand as he shuts the door behind me.

"What if they lock me away?"

"You killed a man who was hunting you. They're not going to lock you away. Trust me."

"I killed someone."

He stops and cups my jaw. "You saved our lives, you survived, they will not lock you away for that."

We take a few steps and I study the people, waiting for one of them to say something. Nobody does. They just move past us as if we're any old person on the street. They don't care. Why should they? We're last week's news. Bigger and better things have happened since us, and nobody is worried about it anymore. At least, that's what I'm telling myself.

We move to the crossing and a familiar sound rings through the warm day, filling my ears and making my body go stiff. It starts as a low hum and quickly gets louder and louder. I hear it above the cars. Above the buses. Above the chatter of people walking past. Everything else fades into nothing as it gets louder and louder. My body freezes, my ears ring, my skin prickles, and I can't move.

"Lara." Noah's voice is a warm rush in my ear. "It's just a motorcycle. He's not here."

He's not here.

"He's dead. You're okay."

Dead.

Okay.

I focus. In front of me, stopped at the lights, is a young man on a motorcycle, eyes ahead, probably just traveling to work.

"It's not him," Noah says softly into my ear. "You're okay."

"I'm . . . I'm sorry," I whisper.

"Don't be sorry. You have nothing to be sorry about. It's going to take some time. Let's get you inside."

When the traffic clears, he leads me across the road and into the police station. I exhale the second we're behind closed doors and gather myself.

I saw a therapist yesterday for the first time, and she told me this was normal: A lot of people suffer post-traumatic stress after facing a horrifying ordeal. We'd work through it over time.

"Lara, Noah, welcome."

I look up to see a man I've come to know as Sergeant Walters. He's been leading the investigation and called us in here today.

We both move toward him. "Sergeant," Noah says, shaking his hand. "What can we do for you?"

"Come, take a seat."

We follow him into his office and sit down, taking a seat in front of his desk.

"Sorry to call you in here, but my team has found the body of Bryce after we determined his location from the details you provided."

I shiver.

It's a relief, sure, but it also makes things more real.

"Unfortunately, we've been unable to locate the cave you told us about and we were wondering if you would be able to help us. We can't get choppers low enough to see anything so the men are going on foot. It's very difficult."

My body freezes. Help them. They want us to go back.

"You want us to go back?" Noah grates out.

"I wouldn't ask if I didn't have to, believe me. I understand how horrific it must have been to be in there, but those teens have families who need answers, too."

"No," I cry, launching out of my seat. "No, I won't do it."

I turn and run out the door, hearing Noah calling my name. I round the corner into the reception area where I see Maggie, the woman who picked me up that night, on the floor, her head in her hands, sobbing hysterically. I come to an abrupt stop as I watch her body shake. Her husband, Peter, leans down, curling his arms around her, crying too. What are they doing here?

"Please," she begs to no one in particular. "I need to find her. I need to put her to rest. My baby. I know she's gone, I know it in my heart. But she deserves to be put to rest with God, somewhere beautiful. *Please.*"

My feet are frozen to the floor as she breaks. She just breaks.

One of those teenagers is Maggie and Peter's child?

I can't move.

I can't.

"We're doing everything we can to find their bodies, ma'am," an officer says, kneeling down. "The woods are very dense, and there are miles of territory to cover."

"You're not doing everything you can," she screams, her face streaked with tears. "You need to bring in more officers. You need to bring her back from that awful place."

She wants her child home.

A child who didn't get a second chance like me.

A child who barely lived.

I didn't kill him for nothing. I didn't escape only to fall into another pit of fear and horror. I escaped because I'm strong. I escaped because I wanted to live. Those kids didn't escape. They never got the chance to discover who they were. They never got to live. Now I have the chance to reunite them with their families so that they can at least be put to rest properly.

Nan's words repeat in my head, filling my heart with a strength I was allowing to slip again. *"You're all of those things and more, Lara. You're the kindest girl I know. Look how often you come over here and look after me. You're the bravest girl I know. I admit you're a little too loud sometimes, but you go into the world fighting and that makes you something else. You are more than loyal, we both know that. Mostly you're strong. The strongest girl I know. You could endure anything, anything at all. I believe it with all that I am. Be all those things, Lara, and the world will give you what you need."*

I'm moving before I can think about it, kneeling down in front of the broken couple who helped us in our time of need. She looks up and gasps. I reach for her hands and whisper, "I'm going to go back, and I'm going to find your baby for you. I'm going to make sure you get to bring her home."

She sobs and clutches me. "You've been through enough, dear. I couldn't . . ."

"I know what it was like out there," I say,

squeezing her hand. "And without you, we might have never made it to the hospital. Please, let me do this for you."

Peter reaches out and closes his hand over mine. "Thank you," he whispers. "You're so incredibly brave. I don't know if it was meant to be that we found you that night. We were just out looking for our daughter. Then you were there and the rest of the story fell into place . . ."

I stand, swallowing the thick lump in my throat. Maybe he's right. Maybe they found us for a reason, and that reason is so I can return their baby home and they can have a proper good-bye. "I'll do all I can. I'll get her home."

Maggie nods and sobs. "T-t-t-thank you."

I turn and see Noah staring at me with such love and admiration. I smile shakily and walk over to him, taking his hand. "I'm going back in."

He cups my face. "You never cease to amaze me, baby. You're the strongest, most incredible, bravest person I've ever met. I love you."

I lean forward, pressing my forehead against his. "I love you, too."

He turns to the sergeant. "Let's get those kids home to their families."

THIRTY-THREE

My boots crunch over the slowly drying leaves as I take the first step into the forest where I spent over a week of my life living in pure torment. Something strange washes over my body as I walk; it's not peace, but acceptance. I don't look around. I don't focus on anything but the path in front of me. I don't look at the motorcycle marks embedded in the mud, or the broken trees and dangling cameras that have been pulled down.

I just walk.

I need to bring those kids home to their families.

Noah is behind me and I can feel his fear and anxiety radiating through my body. With each step we move into that forest, we remember more. I keep my shoulders squared and keep reminding myself that Bryce is gone, he can't hurt us anymore. I can't let those kids rot in that cave, I can't let their families hurt. If I can bring one good thing out of this, I can make sure they get home for the burial they deserve.

"This path was created by him," I say to Sergeant Walters. "He was quite clever, really."

"Indeed, his plan must have taken years to figure out."

"He put the coconut trees there. Enough to give us food, but food we had to work hard for."

"You two are incredibly brave for surviving."

I shrug, focusing straight ahead. "We did what we had to."

"Run, Lara. Run!"

I can almost hear Noah's voice calling to me through the trees, even now. As we move closer to the stream that became our lifeline, I notice so much more than I did before. All the birds, the sounds, the way the trees link together, the vines we could have used. So much. So simple. Now I'm looking at it without fear. As we reach the stream, I count the coconuts that have fallen to the ground. Eight, to be exact.

Our footprints have solidified in the mud beside the water.

I kneel down and run my fingers over them, closing my eyes and remembering.

It takes me well over an hour to complete this, and then I have to very carefully come back, stepping as close to the edge of the track as I can, making sure I cover every one of my new footprints so he doesn't figure out what I've done. It takes me a good long while to get back to Noah, and when I get there, I find him slumped against a tree, head dropped, eyes closed.

I run forward. Fear clogging my throat.

"Noah!" I scream, dropping to my knees in front of him.

I take his shoulders and shake, panic gripping my chest. No.

His eyes flutter open. I make a strangled, relieved noise.

"I was just resting, Lara," he croaks.

Tears burst forth; I have zero control over them. They tumble down my cheeks in rivers. "I thought . ... for a second I thought . . ."

He reaches up, gripping my chin. "I'm okay. I'll be okay."

I nod, sniffling, trying to suck back my sobs. Noah's fingers move to my jaw and then glide up until he's cupping my face. "We're going to get out of here."

I don't know if I believe that anymore.

"Lara?" Noah calls. I look up at him.

The three officers behind us are letting me have my moment, standing back respectfully.

"We need to follow this stream down. It could take a while, but it's how we found the cave."

"How did you know the cave would be in there?" Walters asks.

"We took a guess. It seemed like a logical thing and it paid off."

"That's clever thinking."

I shrug. "Not really. He knew about it. For a while, though, it gave us hope."

I glance at Noah and our eyes lock. Understanding.

"A moment before we go into the stream?" Noah asks.

Walters nods and he and the other two men find a log to sit on. Noah comes over to me, cupping my face in his hands. "You're incredible, the way you're leading this search, the strength you're showing. I know how hard it is to be back here. I feel it, I hear it, I breathe it, and all I want to do is run. But seeing you, so fucking brave . . ."

I lean up on my tiptoes and kiss him, long and deep. When I pull back, I whisper, "I got my second chance here, Noah. Those kids didn't. It isn't about me."

"You take my breath away," he whispers, stroking his thumb over my cheek. "Just like the first night I met you. You had me hooked then, and you have me hooked now."

"Except this time, I'm not going to be stupid enough to let you go," I breathe, cupping his jaw with my hand.

"I'd never let you run again. I should have chased you harder. I should have fought harder."

"We've had our fight, we've had our chase, now let's just keep us."

"Deal," he murmurs, kissing me again before waving the men over.

I step into the water and we move, far more

easily now than we did last time we were here. It takes us a few hours to reach the big pool before the cave. I stop, legs carefully flailing around in the water as I keep myself from going under. The officers are behind us, also in the water. I am sure the other entrance to the cave would be far drier, but we never did see where it emerged.

"I can't go any farther," I say. "I don't think I can handle seeing them, but that's the cave in there. We'll wait for you on the side."

"We understand," Harry, the kind officer who was with us from the start, says.

"Just go up and walk through that waterfall," Noah offers. "We'll wait by the stream."

They nod and disappear into the waterfall. I swim to the edge and climb out into the all-too-familiar clearing and sit, running my fingers over the soft, dry earth.

"Are you okay?" Noah asks, sitting beside me.

"We made it out," I say. "Against all odds we made it out. There were so many times I honestly believed we wouldn't. I very nearly gave up because I thought we had no chance. But here we are."

"Here we are," he says, taking my hand. "Your nan would be so fucking proud of you right now."

My bottom lip trembles and he reaches over, taking my hand.

"She would, Lara. She believed in you more than anyone I know. She would be telling everyone she knew you'd make it if she were here."

I laugh weakly. "She would. She'd be proud.

You're right, she would be glad to see that I've found myself again, but I didn't do it for Nan. I did it for you."

"It took a lot of guts. I'll be forever thankful," he says, his voice a low rasp.

"I don't think I'll ever fully forgive myself for what happened to Nan, but I've accepted it and I've learned from it. I push a huge part of myself down because of what happened, and part of it was my fault, but the other part was just being in the wrong place at the wrong time, with horrible people. Just like the situation we were in. Sometimes you can't control fate, no matter what you do. I never should have buried who I am. I should have simply learned a lesson and bettered myself."

"You're doing that now. That's all that matters."

I snuggle closer to him. "There were so many times I thought we'd never get out of here, and now here we are sitting back in the place that was our nightmare."

"It's beautiful, isn't it?"

"It's so fucking beautiful."

"He honestly thought he had us pegged," Noah says, gliding his thumb over my open palm that's resting in his hand. "He was so sure he knew how this would go, how we'd act."

"We proved him wrong."

Noah squeezes my hand. "We proved him wrong."

EPILOGUE

2 years later

I smile over at Noah, who is holding our daughter. She's gurgling as she looks up at him, chubby hands waving around. I move closer to them, stopping at the back of the couch and leaning over, pressing a kiss to his neck and then reaching down and taking Bethy's hand, letting her curl her tiny fingers around mine. She has her daddy's eyes. In fact, she is all of him.

Perfection.

"You're not going to the station today?" I say, pressing my nose to his neck and breathing him in.

He sighs. "No, got a day home with my girls."

"Hmmm, I wonder how we can spend that?"

He growls and turns, pressing his lips against mine. "That'll all depend on your daughter."

"My daughter?" I giggle. "So she's mine when she's being naughty, but yours when she's good?"

He grins. "Exactly."

I reach for the remote and flick the television on, seeing a news report pop up. It's the same story that has been on for the last few weeks. It's swarming every television and magazine in the country.

"This again," Noah says, his voice tight.

"Yeah," I murmur, letting him go and moving around the couch to sit down beside him. "I don't understand why anyone would want to make themselves famous for living through such an ordeal."

His body tightens. "Neither do I. I'd happily spend the rest of my life never thinking about what happened in that forest, let alone writing a book about it."

I cross my legs and watch the screen. A young girl, Marlie Jacobson, was recently taken by a serial killer dubbed the Watcher near Denver, Colorado. It was said that she escaped after killing him. It's what happened afterward that really shocked the world. She went from a nobody to a famous author overnight when a book was released about her ordeal and she made millions.

"I heard her mother was behind the book," I say, watching intently. "Look how broken she looks."

The girl on the screen is walking down the street, head down, her mother following close behind her, smiling and waving at the cameras. The girl has a distinct limp; from what I read, the killer broke her knees. She's not very old. And from my own experience, living through something like that is a damned nightmare. I wish I could take her into my arms and tell her it'll be okay. Nobody deserves to live through that.

"She doesn't look happy," Noah says, his eyes on the screen. "That's for sure."

"Why would any mother want to make money from her child's heartbreak?"

Noah shrugs, running his hand absently through Bethy's hair. "It's pretty fucked up."

"Poor girl," I say, lifting the remote and flicking the television off. "Could you imagine reliving that horror over and over every time someone brings up her book? It's hard enough to move on. We both know that."

Noah's eyes find mine and he smiles. I smile back. Two years later and the memory of Bryce still lives in our minds, but we've found a way to live with it. It took a lot of time and therapy for us to get back to living even a remotely normal life, but we managed.

Bethy coming along has made things so much better for us. She brings light into our lives. She reminds us why we fought. She reminds us that there is happiness after darkness.

"Knock knock!"

We both turn to see Maggie and Peter coming in. Maggie has a freshly baked cake in her hands, which she promptly hands to Peter as she rushes forward, scooping our daughter out of Noah's hands.

"How's my little baby girl?" she croons.

I can't help the smile that spreads across my face. After we found Maggie and Peter's daughter and they laid her to rest, we all became close. It seemed inevitable. Maggie is like my nan in so many ways, I wonder at times if she's Nan's way of making sure I'm okay. Maybe she's Nan's forgiveness. Maybe she's my forgiveness. I've learned over time to free myself from guilt over Nan's death, and instead learn from it and better myself. I also want to ensure I am the best version of myself for my daughter.

We named our daughter after Maggie's daughter, which just felt right.

Having them in our lives just feels right.

"She's been keeping her mama awake." I smile, tucking myself into Noah's side when he stands.

We both watch Maggie fussing over Bethy and I know his heart is swelling as big as mine. Peter comes over and croons to Bethy now, too. They look like doting grandparents. Their eyes are light. For these moments, their bodies aren't tense with the pain of losing their own daughter.

Their daughter can never be replaced, but that hole in their hearts is slowly being filled with every passing second they spend with Bethy.

I said I wanted to give back to the world, and there were so many times I wondered how I'd do that.

Then Bethy was born and I knew exactly how I could do that.

Watching this couple who has lost so much with Bethy is like watching my nan with me.

A beautiful bond being re-created.

My way of giving back, of making the future better than the past.

Just the way it should be.

Don't miss Bella Jewel's next thrilling romantic suspense!

THE WATCHER

Coming in 2017

From St. Martin's Press